Hellfire

Leesa Gazi is a British-Bangladeshi writer, actor, scriptwriter and filmmaker. She's also the joint artistic director of a London based arts company, Komola Collective. She was the scriptwriter and performer on *Six Seasons* and *A Golden Age* at the Southbank Centre, London. Gazi's recent play *Aleya Twist* is a Bengali adaptation of the British classic *Oliver Twist*. It has reimagined Oliver Twist as a young girl. Gazi also wrote, directed and produced several CVE (Counter Violence Extremism) short films for a UK-based Counter-Extremism think tank in 2017 and 2019.

Gazi was the concept-developer, co-writer and performer on *Birangona: Women of War*, nominated for The Offies 2014, which she later developed into the documentary film called *Rising Silence*, on the lives of rape survivors in the aftermath of the Liberation War of Bangladesh. The film won the Best Documentary Award 2019 at the Dhaka International Film Festival, the 2019 Moondance Winner in the feature documentary category (USA), the Asian Media Award for Best Investigation 2019 (UK), the Award Of Merit 2020 by the Accolade Competition (USA), the Best Documentary Feature and Best Message at the 2020 Top Indie Film Awards (Japan) and the Best Feature—Foreign 2020 at the Queen Palm International Film Festival (USA). Gazi has recently translated Ben Musgrave's new play, *Indigo Giant*, set against the backdrop of the Indigo Rebellion in Bengal during the British Raj, into

Bengali (*Neel Chhaya*) for an international theatrical tour in 2021. Her debut novel, *Rourob*, was published in 2010.

Shabnam Nadiya is a California-based Bangladeshi writer and translator. A graduate of the Iowa Writers' Workshop, she is the recipient of the Schulze Fellowship (2013) at the Iowa Writers' Workshop; the Steinbeck Fellowship at San Jose State University (2019) for her novel-in-progress *Unwanted*; and a PEN/Heim Translation Grant (2020) for her translated manuscript of Bangladeshi writer Mashiul Alam's short fiction. Her translation of Mashiul Alam's story, 'Milk', won the 2019 Himal Southasian Short Story Contest.

Nadiya's published translations include Moinul Ahsan Saber's novel *The Mercenary* (Bengal Lights Books, 2016; Seagull Books, 2018) and Shaheen Akhtar's novel *Beloved Rongomala* (Bengal Lights Books, 2018). Her own writing as well as her translations have been widely published in journals and anthologies such as *The Offing*, *Joyland*, Amazon's *Day One*, *Gulf Coast*, *Copper Nickel*, *Wasafiri*, *Words Without Borders*, *Asymptote*, *Al Jazeera Online* and *Flash Fiction International* (WW Norton). The manuscript of this translation of Leesa Gazi's debut novel *Hellfire* was shortlisted for the Käpylä Translation Prize.

'This incredible novel confirms Leesa Gazi as the most exciting and original voice in contemporary Bangladeshi literature ... It's a study in atmosphere, almost unbearably tense, with a gripping twist of an ending. This is Gazi's debut novel, translated impeccably by Shabnam Nadiya, and it has haunted my dreams ever since I turned the first page'

—Tahmima Anam, author of *A Golden Age*

'A stark and compelling evocation of how the need to keep a tight check by a family—or a society—can unravel in the course of a single day'

—*The Wire*

'A scintillating novel that will keep you engrossed from beginning to end while you ride the waves of surprise, pity, laughter, empathy, fear, and shock'

—*Dhaka Tribune*

'In its terrifying realness, *Hellfire* offers a convincing counterpoint to trigger warnings in art'

—*Open*

'A thrilling, unsettling and wildly satisfying descent into the macabre'

—*Scroll.in*

'Fluid and compelling'

—*Huffpost*

'Gazi's novel not only takes the reader into the deepest recesses of a family's present and past, but also holds up a mirror to a profoundly broken society'

—*Mint*

'This disturbing thriller with its cautionary tale against authoritarian behaviour and uncritical obeisance to convention, shows us how excessive control contains the seeds of its own collapse'

—The Asian Age

'The most shocking novel I read last year ... It crushed me because such living arrangements do exist'

—The Book Satchel

'A dark, thought-provoking page-turner with a chilling denouement'

—Hindustan Times

'A pointed examination of toxic family ties, faith and social hierarchy'

—The Hindu

HELLFIRE

LEESA GAZI

TRANSLATED FROM THE BENGALI BY
SHABNAM NADIYA

eka

eka

First published in Bengali as *Rourob* in 2010 by Sucheepatra

Published in English as *Hellfire* in 2020 by Eka, an imprint of Westland Publications Private Limited

Published in 2024 by Eka, an imprint of Westland Books, a division of Nasadiya Technologies Private Limited

No. 269/2B, First Floor, 'Irai Arul', Vimalraj Street, Nethaji Nagar, Alapakkam Main Road, Maduravoyal, Chennai 600095

Westland, the Westland logo, Eka and the Eka logo are the trademarks of Nasadiya Technologies Private Limited, or its affiliates.

ISBN: 9789360455828

10 9 8 7 6 5 4 3 2 1

Typeset by Jojy Philip, New Delhi

Printed at Parksons Graphics Pvt. Ltd

Lovely adored wandering random streets without purpose. Getting out of the house, however, was a task as hard and complicated as crossing the *pulserat*, that final bridge of the afterlife spanning the fires of hell. But today was different; today she had left home all by herself, alone. Only Allah ta'ala Himself knew how this impossible had become possible today.

It wasn't as if she never went out. But it was always with their mother; though once or twice, she had gone out with just Beauty. Those were memorable days. Today she had come out all by herself to buy fabric for shalwar-kameez. Incredible, but true.

Of course, their mother Farida Khanam had, as usual, insisted that she take Beauty with her. The surprising thing was that even though Beauty hadn't come with her in the end, Farida Khanam hadn't stopped Lovely from going out. Who could explain this sudden change of heart?

It was Farida Khanam who had initially proposed the trip. 'If you want to go to Gausia Market, get going. Go and see if Beauty wants to come along. Her majesty, the queen, is still in bed, faking sleep.'

Lovely had banged fruitlessly on Beauty's door. No response. This was a problem; once her royal highness fell asleep, it was an accomplishment for her to wake up. It was only nine in the morning. Beauty usually began to stir only around ten or ten thirty. Even after she was up, there were various faddish beauty routines to be observed. Beyond the usual teeth-brushing and face-washing, she had additional habits that took up at least an hour. She parted her hair precisely in the middle and brushed each side with exactly one hundred strokes. Then she either left her hair loose or wove it into a tight, long braid. The refrigerator always had some fresh lentil paste ready for her. Beauty smeared the paste on her face and sat with it for at least half an hour. When the crushed lentil dried and became brittle, she soaked a washcloth in hot water, wrung it out, and, slowly and thoroughly, wiped her face with it. Lovely was pretty sure that there was no way to get her ready before noon. Still, she tried to wake Beauty up because Farida Khanam had ordered her to. It didn't work.

'Amma, Beauty's still asleep.'

'*Namaj nai, kalam nai—shudhu ghoom* ... No praying, no reading the holy book—all she ever does is sleep. There's no point in rousing her anyway; she'll just settle herself in front of the mirror. Go and get ready. Check with her again before you leave—see if she wants to go then.'

Lovely didn't have many needs. She neither sat down to part her hair like Beauty, nor did she spread lentil paste on her face. She did her hair in a slapdash manner, fixing it in her usual style—two long plaits. As she braided her hair, Lovely noticed that she had split ends. Her hair was long enough to reach below her back, but it ended in rattails. She would have to ask Beauty to snip the ends off. She soaped her face. Soap seemed to dry out her face these days. It wasn't like this before. Lovely pondered this as she rubbed her face with Nivea cream. She needed to use face cream only in the winter. She didn't need it in the summer. Lovely opened the dresser drawer and pulled out the first kameez her eyes fell on.

She was desperately hoping that Farida Khanam wouldn't come with them today. There was no good reason for her wish. Whether Farida Khanam went with them or not wouldn't really make much difference. At most, the two sisters would eat some chotpoti or fuchka together. They could still do that with their mother there. But when it was just the two of them, Lovely felt a different kind of ease.

It took her barely ten minutes to get ready. But Beauty completely refused to go with her. Who knew what she was doing in there with her door locked. Lovely felt miserable. Farida Khanam banged on Beauty's door a few times, trying to get her to open up, but she too failed.

'She's a curse, that girl,' Farida Khanam exclaimed in annoyance. 'One sister's like a gape-jawed fish, dying to go out of the house every single second, and the other one won't budge even if you beat her up.'

No matter how it had worked out, the end of the story was that Lovely was now walking down the street all by herself, wondering how this incredible thing had happened. This easily qualified as an entry in the Guinness Book of World Records.

Today was her birthday; she had just turned forty. Perhaps that was why their mother had let her go out by herself. A couple of CNG three-wheelers drove by. Lovely almost hailed one but didn't. She would just walk for a little while. Of course, if someone spotted her it would be reported back home. That boy servant of theirs was tiny, but the devil incarnate. He was constantly badmouthing the two of them to Amma. Just as Lovely was thinking to herself, give me a chance and I'll teach that imp such a lesson, he'll go straight for the rest of his life, a three-wheeler stopped right beside her.

'Get in, apa. I'll take you to Gausia.'

Lovely spun around. Just as she had thought. The little devil was standing at a distance with all his teeth bared in a grin. Amma had sicced him on her. Lovely just wanted to die. She raised her hand, miming a slap to the boy, and climbed into the three-wheeler. It was now ten o'clock, and she had to be back before lunchtime. She felt relieved. This was the first time that Amma hadn't given her a specific time. She had only said, be back by lunchtime. Which meant that the next few hours, until two o'clock, belonged to her. She began praying that they wouldn't get stuck in traffic. The three-wheeler was speeding ahead, as fast as it could.

What a surprise! By ten forty-five, Lovely was at Gausia. She climbed out of the three-wheeler, paid the fare, and stood for a few minutes like a fool. She couldn't figure out what to do, which way to go. She could walk to Chandni Chowk or she could head towards Gausia Market. Suddenly, Lovely felt very lonely. The man inside her head took this chance to speak up. His voice sounded broken, pleading: ('Apumoni, my sweet sister, apni emon keno bolen toh? Why are you like this? Come on, just buy some fabric, fast, and then let's go pass the time by the Buriganga river. Just you and me.')

No, Lovely wasn't prepared to pay attention to the man inside her head right now. She was going to shop as much as she wanted today. Then she would stand somewhere and eat some chotpoti, maybe drink a lassi; or maybe she wouldn't.

Step by step, she moved towards Chandni Chowk. Because it was only a quarter to eleven, the usual woman-crushing crowds had not gathered yet. No worries; give it an hour and they would show up. The crowd was already pretty bad.

Today she had travelled somewhere all by herself. Lovely couldn't remember the last time she had gone anywhere by herself. Had she *ever* gone anywhere by herself? She gave up. She felt annoyed at her own foolishness. Was she going to let these banal thoughts occupy her at this moment she had yearned for?

She entered a fabric store at random. The trouble was that she liked every single fabric she saw. Of course, no matter what fabric she chose, it wouldn't suit her. There was already an aunty-like air about her. Who knew what had possessed her to show up at Chandni Chowk in these long braids. She must look like a clown. People were passing her by, for sure, but many stopped a few steps away and turned back to look her up and down. A pair of untidy braids, the hem of her kameez trailing a handspan below her knees, scruffy eyebrows, a lost, dazed look in her eyes, the sweetness of her mien disappearing with desperate speed. Such a creature wasn't spotted too often in the Dhaka markets. Here she stood waiting, holding a bolt of cloth for such a long time, yet even the salesman wasn't paying any attention to her. Lovely's eyes teared up.

'Hey, bhai, how much is this per yard? Hey, listen, bhai, please, listen ...'

'Which one? You've got a different fabric in each hand.'

'The red one.'

'A hundred and twenty takas.'

'Okay, give me two and a half yards of this, and matching fabric for the shalwar and the orna.'

'I can give you the shalwar, but you'll have to buy the orna from a different shop. We don't sell ornas unless they're part of a set. How much fabric do you want for the shalwar?'

'Two and a half yards.'

The salesman busied himself with measuring and cutting. What sort of customer came to shop at Chandni Chowk but didn't bother to haggle? He gave her the once over as he cut the cloth to measure. She looked a little stupid.

'Here you go. I'm charging you one hundred and ten takas per yard. You didn't haggle at all, so I'm giving you a small discount.'

Lovely paid and left the store. She didn't even like red that much, why on earth had she bought it? Beauty liked red though. Beauty loved all the vivid colours. Lovely walked into a couple of other stores and walked right out. She didn't feel like buying an orna now. She would come back for the orna at some later date with their mother. That would make Amma happy. Farida Khanam was constantly trying to prove how useless the two of them were without her help. Lovely's inability to buy an orna would be further proof of their uselessness. It could be assumed with some degree of certainty that she would not approve of the fabric. No matter what it was the sisters did in Farida Khanam's absence, it was impossible to convince her that they had done anything right.

In her mind, Lovely flew back twenty-six years. The man inside her head gasped: ('Please, Apumoni, don't rush like that. It makes me dizzy.')

——

Although Lovely was three years older than Beauty, they were students in the same class. Lovely had been fourteen at the time. Farida had gone out, leaving her daughters in the custody of her husband, Mukhles shaheb. She was headed for Chowdhury Para, Khilgaon, where her older sister Rahela lived. The prospective marriage of Rahela's second daughter, Ruma, was under discussion. Farida wasn't inclined to spend too much time at Rahela's since she had left her daughters behind. She also had to stop and pick up some fresh produce on her way back. There were no vegetables in the house. All she could find in the kitchen before she left home were a couple of dried-up, dreary looking eggplants. Mukhles shaheb had been unwell for the last few days and had been unable to do the groceries. She had to buy vegetables as well as flour. That morning she had barely managed to scrape together a dozen rutis for breakfast. Farida kept her brows furrowed the entire way as she sat inside the three-wheeler. She felt uneasy. She had to get back home as soon as she could.

Mukhles shaheb was burning up with fever. Before leaving the house, their mother had sternly instructed Lovely and Beauty not to make any noise. Their father was in bed with the covers drawn up over his head. His headache was killing him. Other than the three of them in the house, there was the old maidservant whom they called *bua*, and Sultana, the young maidservant. Sultana was about the same age as the two of them. Sultana didn't dare come anywhere near them when Farida Khanam was home. Their mother was very strict about that. Servants should know their place. There was no call to be extra friendly with them.

Lovely took some spring chicken soup to her father, and then settled down to play Snakes and Ladders with Beauty. She inevitably lost to her sister. There were some instances when Lovely had managed to win a game of Ludo. But with Snakes and Ladders, as soon as she sat down to play, she got swallowed by the snakes.

Beauty, of course, was an avid player. There was pleasure in witnessing Lovely's game piece suffer snakebites and writhe its way down to the bottom of the board. Beauty grew bug-eyed with joy.

'Apa, do you want to go to the roof?' asked Sultana.

'Shut up. Do you want to play Snakes and Ladders? Come, sit here,' said Lovely.

'No, I don't want to play, I want to go to the roof,' said Sultana.

'What do you mean you want to go to the roof? How can you do that? The roof's locked,' Beauty said.

'No, it's not,' Sultana reported, as if divulging a state secret.

'Bua will tell Amma,' Lovely said.

'Bua is asleep. She's not going to wake up so soon,' Beauty said.

'Beauty, I'm warning you, don't you dare. Amma told us not to go up there,' Lovely cautioned.

'Amma's not going to see us. I'm going to go up. You don't have to come if you don't want to.'

'If you want to go, you better do it now,' said Sultana. 'We'll just stay there for a little bit and come down. Not a single soul will know.'

Sultana's solemnity made Lovely a little bolder. 'Wait, let me go and check on Abba.'

'What's there to check? Abba's a no-account anyway.'

Lovely paid no attention to Beauty. She tiptoed over to Mukhles shaheb's room and peeked inside. He was fast asleep; she could hear his light snore. The three of them peeked into the kitchen and saw Bua comfortably asleep on a mat. Lovely's heart was going a mile a minute. The three of them held hands and crept to the front door. Beauty held her breath as she pulled it open. It creaked on rusted hinges. In the silence of that afternoon, even that small noise froze them, like trees struck by lightning.

Beauty was the first to recover. 'Are we just going to wait by the door? Come on!'

Silent, but with laughter bubbling through their bodies like boiling water, the three of them snuck up to the roof. As soon as they opened the door and walked out, their laughter exploded. A crow flew off the ledge. Lovely would never forget that moment when they stepped onto the roof—that excitement, that joy!

She could no longer remember how long they had stayed up there. All she remembered was Amma's face, her standing there stock-still, like a nightmare.

Farida Khanam didn't say a single word to either of them. Sultana and Bua were sacked right away. She didn't even say a single word to her husband. As if she had already known that her absence would lead to something like that. She understood, down to her bones, just how important her decision to cancel her visit to her sister's house had been.

The torments of the grave were visited upon the sisters. They had to move again. This time Farida Khanam had found a permanent solution. She sold off the plot of land in Pallabi that she had inherited from her father, and built a small, two-story house in the interior of Monipuripara. She shouldered the entire responsibility for the construction. They moved into the house before it was even finished.

Since then, Farida Khanam had never employed a young girl as a maidservant. Instead, she hired boys between the ages of eight to ten. They got the job when they were eight and were dismissed as soon as they reached thirteen.

Lovely pulled out a corner of the red fabric from the brown paper bag. It was quite nice actually, there was no reason to dislike it. It was a bit too red though. She shouldn't have bought red for the shalwar as well. Like the poem, *Laley lal duniya*, this world made red by red.

('*Oh, mother, your babe has been killed by the killer.*') The man inside her head supplied the second line. He went silent after that, but it jolted Lovely.

Even when they were small children, both sisters knew that Farida Khanam waited outside the school gate while their class was in session. It wasn't a problem when they were very small. But when they reached Class Three, the school principal wouldn't tolerate it anymore. One day, she summoned Farida Khanam.

'*Assalamalaikum.*'

'*Walaikum Assalam.*'

'You're the mother of Lovely and Beauty.'

'Yes.'

'I heard from our doorman that you wait outside the gate every day after school starts.'

'Yes, I do.'

'Why?'

'My daughters are in there and I'm just supposed to leave and go home?'

'Do any of the other mothers wait outside the entire time?'

'But I'm not bothering you. I just stand outside the gate. My daughters are in there. They might need something.'

'Please, just drop them off here and leave. Then come and pick them up at dismissal. There's no need to wait outside. We'll take care of anything they need.'

'My daughters are very shy. They won't ask even if they need something.'

'It makes no difference if they don't. They'll be able to tell you in a few hours anyway. Don't wait outside anymore.'

After that, for almost a year, they didn't go to any school at all. Farida Khanam persuaded her husband to move them to a different house. They rented an apartment directly across from Shajahanpur Girls' School. They moved into the third floor, and thus began Farida's balcony vigil. The entire time the girls were in school, she stood unmoving in the front balcony, grasping the iron grille. Then, once the distant sound of the dismissal bell reached her ears, she slowly descended the stairs. Even slower, she crossed the street. When the girls emerged from the school gate and looked at her with fearful eyes, she would smile and hold out her hands. The girls sighed in relief. The same thing every single day. The same routine every single day. As immutable as the laws of nature.

—

Lovely almost stumbled over a pebble. She had, without even noticing, left Chandni Chowk and walked over to the cinema hall. The enormous billboard was overwhelmed by the even more enormous movie star, her unconstrained flesh bursting out of the advertisement.

Lovely began to pay attention to the girls around her. Whenever she went outside these days, she wondered at the number of pretty girls living in the city. Everyone had to have their own beauty regimens these days. It had also become trendy to go to beauty salons. Should she visit one today? Or she could even pop into the movie theatre!

Of course, if Amma found out, she would murder Lovely. Somehow or other, that woman found out everything.

A girl just like Lovely was standing nearby. Although Lovely no longer had the nerve to call herself a girl. After all, she had turned forty today. How strange! Forty years had gone by, and yet she had nothing; she hadn't even been married. Suddenly the girl made eye contact with her and smiled sweetly. Lovely immediately glanced behind her. Only then was she sure that the girl had indeed smiled at her. She turned towards her, smiling back, but by then the girl had looked away. Lovely decided to follow the girl. If the girl went into the theatre by herself, she would enter too. She would sit beside the girl, and the two of them would have fun watching the movie together. They could chat about this and that. When she got back home, she would relish spinning out stories about her new friend to Beauty.

She hadn't noticed when a college student sporting a thin moustache had come to stand beside the girl. Fancy guy. He was wearing an elaborate orange *fatua* with some yellow lettering on it. Men these days flaunted such colours. Lovely had never seen her father wear anything other than various shades of blue or white. Although her cousin Riaz often wore maroon shirts. That too was many years ago. Riaz lived in Germany now, with his pretty, foreign wife and their two children.

Lovely felt uneasy without even realising it. The boy and the girl were talking with their heads lowered. They were probably talking about her. The boy glanced at Lovely for a moment. The girl's lips were flapping fast. Who knew what she was telling the boy? The boy cocked an eyebrow and then stuck his tongue out in a lewd manner. Maybe he was laughing. Step by step, Lovely moved away from the theatre. She would be fine without ever watching *Bap-Betir Juddho*, the Father-Daughter Battle. At any rate, the 'Mother-Daughter Battle' that she was witnessing in her lifetime seemed to have no end in sight. Of course, no one could say that Lovely had ever disobeyed her mother even unwittingly. But it would be a different story if you considered what went on inside her. She started walking fast. She rushed a long way on unsteady feet, and stopped only when she had crossed the overbridge. She was parched. *Eish*, if only she could find some green coconut water. She would strike a pose by the roadside and sip the water with a straw. Lovely looked around, searching for green coconuts.

Every conceivable thing was being sold on the sidewalk. It was so crowded, it felt like people were about to eat each other's heads. In the middle of all this, in a voice that sounded like he had just woken up, the man inside her head spoke: ('Apumoni, it's almost noon. Why don't we go somewhere, just to hang for a while? Okay, let's go to New Market. I have an idea.')

Lovely felt his cackling spread through her body. She nodded in assent and headed for one of the entrances. It felt like she was going to New Market for a particular errand. The suppressed excitement of the man inside her head began to infect her. She picked up her pace without noticing. She stepped on the sandal of the woman ahead of her; the woman in the ball-print sari stumbled and almost fell but managed to keep herself upright. She spun around and said something to Lovely, teeth bared and face distorted, but Lovely heard nothing. The man was banging away inside her head: thump-thump-thump. The quicker his beat, the quicker her pace.

She walked through the New Market gate and past the blouse shops. She crossed the jumble of snack shops and eateries, then the sari stores, then the jewellery stores. She went farther in. She reached the crockery shops at the very end and paused to breathe. The pounding inside her head instantly stopped. As if someone had been pushing her towards some brave adventure and, placing her life on the line, Lovely had just completed it.

She suddenly felt exhausted, but at the same time, content. Although she couldn't quite tell whether it was contentment or relief. She ambled like a pigeon in front of shops that were dazzling bright with lights.

'Come inside, bhabi. What do you need?'

'No, nothing. I'm just looking ...'

The salesman had addressed her as bhabi, sister-in-law. Lovely felt her insides flood with joy. She desperately wanted to buy something from this particular shop.

('What do you mean you don't need anything? Will you ever get another chance like this? Please, Apumoni, go in.')

'Do you have knives? A knife? A bread knife, or, no, a knife for vegetables?'

'Yes, I do. I have them in different sizes, which kind do you want? Wait a second, bhabi, let me show you a foreign-made knife set.'

'No, no, I don't need a set. Just give me one knife that is medium sharp. You know, I do have to go into the kitchen once in a while, and he hates things like that. I'm talking about my husband. I mean he hates me sitting on the ground like a maidservant with a *boti* to slice vegetables. So give me a knife that would work with meat as well.' As she spoke, Lovely blushed a deep red. She could clearly picture how annoyed her husband was with her. She could hear him say, 'What the hell is this, cutting and chopping on the ground with your legs all spread out like a housemaid?'

'Well, how am I supposed to do this then?'

'Why, haven't you seen on television? You can use knives to chop vegetables quite nicely while standing up. You can even gut fish.'

'Sure, you can gut fish! As if that actually works.'

'Try chopping onions and things like that to start with. Then you'll get the hang of it.'

('Wake up, wake up, Apumoni, up you go—the salesman is dying to show you his thing.') The man snickered inside her head. Lovely's cheeks were burning. What was he saying!

'Bhabi, take a look at this knife, it's a fine one. Foreign product. Look at how sharp it is; you'll find it very convenient to cut meat with.'

'Yes, that one. Give me that one.' Lovely's voice quavered. She sneaked a look around. No, there were no other customers in the shop at the moment. The salesman overcharged her a little. But she had no regrets. The knife was indeed a good one, foreign-made.

The stainless-steel knife slid back into its plastic sheath. When she took the knife from the salesman, their fingers touched. It felt good, very good. Her cheeks and ears began to burn—what was happening!

('It's all good! All good, what's happening here!')

'Shut up, just shut up!' For the first time ever, Lovely berated the man inside her head. He paid no attention and sniggered. She placed the knife very carefully inside her bag.

The salesman watched her with some interest. Weird customers showed up now and then. This woman seemed to be having a whispered conversation with someone invisible, and then she would suddenly startle. Did she have a screw loose?

'Apa, do you need anything else?' he asked.

'Not apa, say bhabi. You were calling me bhabi just now. No, I don't need anything else.'

She left the store on light feet. She felt cheerful. She had pulled off quite a thing. Beauty would never believe it. When she got home, she would have to make a production of showing the knife to Beauty. Of course, if her royal highness had opened her door by then. She had to come out for lunch, though, so she could show it to her then. She would do it as if it was no big deal to carry around a sharp knife in your purse. She would pull it out casually when they were chatting.

Suddenly, Lovely looked back. The salesman was standing outside his shop, staring at her. She whipped her gaze away. She had to get away from here, as quickly as possible. But why? She hadn't done anything wrong. All she had done was buy an innocent knife. Gradually her pace slowed down to normal.

She exited through the New Market gate and stood still. What should she do now? The man inside her head had actually shut up after the first ever scolding she had given him. She needed a plan. Where should she go? There was no question of returning home so soon.

She felt the desire to pull her knife out and gaze at it. She unzipped her purse and out came the knife. It was hidden inside the plastic sheath, and then wrapped with a hundred pieces of tape. As if the salesman had nothing better to do. Didn't he know you weren't supposed to use plastic anymore? Her heart hungered to touch the blade. She ripped at it until the tape was destroyed. She tossed the pieces into the sewage drain by the car park. As soon as the knife slid from the sheath into her hands, the fierce vigour of the winter sun slithered across the stainless-steel blade. The light splashed Lovely's eyes and face like a lit sparkler. Such joy!

('Are you just going to stand here enjoying this beauty or head for Ramna Park?')

Yes, yes, to Ramna Park. She wanted to shout her response to the man inside her head. Had she ever been this happy? Yes, she had. That day when Riaz ...

'Hey, bhai, can you take me to Ramna Park?' Lovely's voice overflowed with joy.

'Sure, just pay me ten takas more than the metre.'

'I will, I will. I'll pay you ten takas more than the metre.' Lovely couldn't recognise herself. Her forty-year-old heart was overshadowed by her eighteen-year-old one.

The CNG three-wheeler made a turn and came to a stop right in front of her. Lovely settled herself comfortably in the back, holding her sling bag on her lap. She really was going to Ramna Park. Who would have thought this could happen to her! But what about the fabric? Where was the packet with the cloth she had just bought? She quickly slipped out of the three-wheeler. She looked this way and that, on the street, inside her bag—she even peeked in the drain. She couldn't find it anywhere. *Eish*, what terrible luck. This was why—this was why her mother never let her go anywhere by herself. She would be allowed to go out alone if she was capable. But where did the package go? She must have left it in the knife store. Should she go back? Lovely felt conflicted.

'What are you looking for?' the driver asked.

'A small packet. It has some fabric in it.'

'Maybe you left it in the shop. You should go back and check there. Was it expensive?'

Another driver stepped forward, followed by another. 'What did she lose? What's going on?'

A young man interjected, 'I watched this apa pull a knife out of her bag, and then she looked up and stared at the sky.'

'Is the knife still there or is that gone too?'

'Where would the knife go? I watched her put the knife back in her bag.'

Lovely felt helpless. She wanted to run away. How awful! That man had even witnessed her moment of intimacy with the knife! What should she do now? Go back to the knife shop and check whether she really had left the package there? Or she could cross the road into Chandni Chowk and just buy the same fabric again. She didn't want to return empty-handed. She didn't want to see her mother's familiar 'didn't I know this already!' smile, not even a bit. Was it true, then, that they, she and her sister, really couldn't get anything done without Farida Khanam? Or was it only Lovely who was useless? Maybe Beauty wasn't this hopeless. Maybe Beauty would have been capable of buying the fabric and getting home as she was supposed to.

Lovely carefully searched her surroundings one more time. Every pair of eyes in the gathered crowd religiously followed her.

'Apa, how much longer can I wait? If you're coming, let's go!'

Lovely gave up. She dragged herself back to the CNG three-wheeler. Several onlookers were annoyed at the driver for putting an end to the spectacle so early.

'*Arrey, mia*, won't you give this apa some time to look? Apa, don't worry, you can get another three-wheeler.'

Lovely almost ran to the three-wheeler. 'Let's get out of this place. Fast!'

The driver was taken aback. He didn't understand the sudden rush, but he started his three-wheeler right away.

He kept glancing at her through his rearview mirror. Once, their eyes met. Should she stick her tongue out at him? The man inside her head snickered. What was the meaning of his laughter? Intolerable! His laughter grew louder and louder until it felt like the inside of the three-wheeler would explode. Lovely felt anxious; there was no way the driver didn't hear that. The ugly laughter rose above the honking and the constant shouting and the burning in her ears and in her brain.

'Shut up, for Allah's sake, just shut up!' she whispered.

('Look inside your bag, Apumoni, your heart will deeeelight!')

Lovely yanked the zipper open even before he had finished talking. Inside was a water bottle, the knife sheathed in plastic, a black coin purse, a yellow journal, and a tiny, pink umbrella. Her aunt had brought the umbrella back from London many years ago. Who knows why her mother had decided to put it in her bag in winter.

('What a pain! Why don't you shove all that crap aside and look?')

After his light scolding, Lovely stuck her hand deep inside. What! The brown package was sitting quietly, way down at the bottom. 'You knew it was inside the bag all this while. Why didn't you tell me?'

('And miss all the fun?')

Lovely tried to be angry at him, but instead, she giggled. She was happy she had found the fabric. She had been saved. Otherwise, she would have to deal with a million and one questions from her mother. And that interrogation would go on for at least a month.

No, she wasn't going to think about Amma or Beauty or home at this moment. She buttoned up her black cardigan and wrapped her shawl tightly around herself. She was feeling a little chilly. The wind was whistling in from both sides of the three-wheeler. Lovely sat in the middle of the seat with her shoulders hunched and her head hung low, like a heron hiding its head. She no longer wanted to have anything to do with this world. The holy prophet received his revelations from the Creator at forty. Which meant that even in the eyes of Allah 'forty' held some special meaning. Something special happened at forty, something special was going to happen today.

As she pondered these doctrinal questions, Lovely realised that whenever she pronounced Allah's name in her head, her thoughts automatically crowded with Arabic and Urdu words. Who knew why! Perhaps Allah wasn't too fond of Bengali. And then, today she hadn't even said her *Fazr* prayers at dawn. Her middle-aged body had felt so heavy when she woke this morning, she couldn't drag it out of bed. Four zero—forty; this thought had kept her numb for a very long time. Still, she shouldn't have missed her prayers. She had got nothing in this lifetime; if she missed out on everything in the afterlife as well, what good would that do? Other than Riaz, her life had enjoyed no light or air.

So, why, after such a long time, was she thinking of Riaz so much today? Riaz was their cousin; his mother was Farida Khanam's youngest sister. She had three sons. Riaz was the eldest. He had been a student at Science College, which was located near their house. He had just started at the college back then; the thin line of his moustache had been barely visible. A full head of slightly wavy hair, thick eyebrows, a tiny scar at the corner of his left eye. Thin, featherweight—he was so dreamy! Lovely used to stroke his scar. He aroused such tenderness in her. Their aunt's house was far away, in Pallabi, so his going home for lunch was out of the question.

Lovely and Beauty had never been close to their cousins on either side. They didn't visit relatives that often, and even when they did, the two of them stuck close to their parents. When they crossed the age of twenty-five, even if their mother went visiting, they stayed back home with their father, although Lovely really wanted to go out with their mother. There were many times she had been desperate to go, but because Beauty didn't feel like going anywhere, Lovely was forced to stay home. By then Farida Khanam felt at ease leaving the two of them behind.

As soon as Farida Khanam would walk out the front door, Mukhles shaheb would lock it with a solemn face. She would wait outside the door; once she heard the key turn in the lock, she would slowly make her way down the stairs. They never strayed from that routine. If someone visited their house when Farida Khanam was out, Mukhles shaheb unlocked the door to let them in. The key ring always hung heavy in the breast pocket of his white shirt. It wasn't as if it was just one key. It was a bunch of about ten: the key to the front door, the key to the iron grille gate at the base of the staircase that led to the second floor, the key to the door to the roof, the keys to the bedrooms of the two sisters, the keys to the two closets, the key to the pantry, and other miscellaneous keys. There were two sets of keys; one for Farida Khanam, the other for Mukhles shaheb.

Their lives had changed drastically after they were caught sneaking to the rooftop when they were fourteen. That was when the Monipuripara house was built. Until that house went up, the two sisters spent their days in harsh imprisonment. If husband and wife went out together, they locked the girls in with the older maidservant. But neither of the parents really felt comfortable with that.

Sometimes they would get halfway to their destination and come back. Sometimes they would go but spend the whole time feeling uneasy. Farida Khanam staked everything she had on building the Monipuripara house, and, even before it was complete, she moved them in.

Even in the new house, just as before, she bound her daughters in the strictest of routines. Still, Farida Khanam could find no relief. Finally, she arrived at a solution. If the girls were not accompanying the two of them somewhere, then husband and wife simply didn't go together. This solution pleased Mukhles shaheb the most. He didn't want to go anywhere anyway. When he came home from work, he huddled in his wicker chair in the bedroom and watched television in a stupor. When he was summoned to dinner, he sat down with everyone else, but that too was in near silence. He never had an opinion on the food served. He ate polao and korma with the same impassivity that he allowed for leftover rice and daal. Farida Khanam was the one who talked a mile a minute at mealtimes. Her daughters kept pace with her. From exhaustive analyses of television dramas to the audacity of the household help—their chatter ranged everywhere. Once in a while, Mukhles shaheb did offer an opinion on television shows, but never with any conviction. Their discussions would hit a peak when their relatives were put on the block. Everyone grew happier in a blink.

—

Riaz and Beauty were three months apart in age; and he was three years younger than Lovely. One afternoon, soon after Riaz began his classes, he visited their house with his mother. Farida Khanam extended a generous invitation to him to come by for lunch now and then. He looked pretty young for his age back then; he was about seventeen, but he looked no older than thirteen or fourteen. And both Lovely and her sister were buxom and sturdy in build. Beauty could even be called fat. Who knew if that was why no improper thoughts entered Farida Khanam's head.

The fact that such misgivings hadn't occurred to her was indeed astonishing. The woman who routinely spotted mountains in molehills blithely arranged for fire and ghee to sit side by side. In her entire life, this was probably the only blunder Farida Khanam had made with regard to her daughters.

('Until this one, today.')

The man inside her head went completely silent after that comment. Lovely exclaimed, 'Meaning?', but there was no response.

It felt so strange to think about it now. Where had Lovely found the nerve? Their mother often chanted the proverb, 'An ant grows wings when it's time to die'. That had to be it; what else could it have been?

That is when it began. Riaz began showing up frequently at their house after his classes. He would eat lunch, address the sisters as *Boro Apa* and *Chhoto Apa*—big sister, little sister—and play endless rounds of Ludo with them. He studied at Science College, but he talked incessantly about the girls at Holy Cross College, which was right next door. As if they were fairytales, Lovely and Beauty didn't merely listen to his stories, they swallowed them whole. Like thirsting birds, they craved Riaz's visits for that whiff of the outside world. Their mother didn't seem to mind. Rather she seemed quite happy when Riaz came. She would quickly fry up some eggplant or make a lentil bharta for lunch. While they played Ludo, she would whip up some jhal-muri, tossing puffed rice with green chillies, shallots and tomatoes. Sometimes, she stood beside them, watching their game with interest.

Lovely could no longer remember precisely when the colour of those games began to change. One morning, she woke up and discovered that if Riaz didn't come that day, she would just die. The shock and joy of this discovery was so intense that as soon as she realised it, she pulled the covers over her head and lay there as if dead, deafened by the hammering of her own heart. She spent that entire day in bed with the excuse that she was feeling unwell. She was praying so hard for Riaz not to come that day that she was foaming at the mouth, while at the same time her mind was slamming itself against a wall, desperate for him to come.

--

The three-wheeler screeched to a stop, halting her winding thoughts. Rather, instead of stopping, her thoughts merely stumbled. Along with her thoughts, Lovely's lowered head almost banged into the iron grille in front of her. A small lock hung from the grille that kept the driver safe from her in a protective enclosure.

('Motherfucking shit! Sorry, Apumoni, I had to curse. So, Mr Riaz seems to be floundering terribly in the ocean of your heart! Hell, this driver guy just poured cold water on it before your story even got to the hot stuff. Get off, get off, go and get some air in the park and think about Mr Riaz for a while, and let me see how far you went with him!')

'Here, apa, did you doze off? We're here. I think you're hurt, maybe. You have to sit tight when the vehicle's moving.'

'No, no, I'm not hurt. What's the fare?'

Lovely *had* banged her head hard. She was rubbing her forehead. It was probably going to swell up to the size of a potato. Trouble only bred more trouble. A swelling on her forehead meant another round of interrogation back home.

('You might be remanded into custody. You might even be finished off in a crossfire.')

'Eighty-two takas.'

Eish, her forehead was throbbing. She was going to get a headache now. Lovely suffered from terrible headaches. Once she got one, she had to lie for hours in a darkened room. What would she do if she got a headache now? She would just have to flop down flat on the grass in Ramna Park.

Lovely took her time unzipping her sling bag. She pulled out her purse and held out a hundred taka note to the driver.

'Here, apa.'

'How much did you give me?'

'Fifteen takas.'

'Why fifteen? Your metre says seventy-one takas and fifty paisa. You asked for an extra ten. You're supposed to take eighty-two takas. Why are you charging me more now?'

'I don't have three takas in change.'

'I'll wait here. You can go and make change.'

'Where am I supposed to get change from?'

'That's not my concern. You have to go.'

('Here we go! Let's see some hoodoo happen.')

'Shut up!'

'Who are you telling to shut up?'

'To the man inside my head. Well, why are you waiting here? Go on and get the change.'

The driver stared at Lovely for a moment. He couldn't decide whether to make trouble or not. It was almost one. He could get at least two more fares by two o'clock before returning the cab and going to eat lunch. If he kicked up a fuss now, it would just waste his time and accomplish nothing. He shouldn't get into a wrangle with this woman who was like a coiled spring. She would sink her claws into him the moment he tried anything.

'Okay, apa, here, take these five takas and go. I don't want the two takas back.'

Lovely climbed out of the three-wheeler quite happily with the twenty takas. As soon as she was out, the winter sun oozed along her body onto the ground. She felt such comfort that she grew drowsy. She wanted to close her eyes and stand still for eternity. When she slowly opened her eyes again, the massive gates of Ramna Park stood right in front of her. The prodding of the man inside her head had finally led her here. Had this been a good idea? She had never ever come to a place like this even with others, let alone all by herself. '*Bismillah*,' she said, before stepping towards the entrance. She flailed in the north wind as she tried to wrap her scarf and her shawl tightly around her. So this was how happiness was supposed to feel!

Beauty would be stunned if she saw her today. This forever-frightened girl, yellowed from being hidden under a rock, was branching out in the warmth of the sun. Her only regret was that she had no wings.

With her head held high, Lovely walked through the park entrance. The enormous trees yearning to reach the sky on either side provided shade. Sunlight broke through after much effort, crossing the dappled shadows to melt onto her skin. Lovely leaned back her head and lifted her face to the sky. A leaf dropped onto her face like a falling star on a dark night. She unzipped her bag with care and placed the leaf inside. Who knew what kind of tree it belonged to. She didn't know anything about plants or trees. It would be good if she knew what tree this came from.

Lovely kept walking straight ahead. After a while, she spotted the lake in the distance, with benches along the banks. She decided to sit quietly on one of the benches. What would happen if she spent the whole afternoon, the whole evening on a bench here before returning home?

('What would happen? World War Three is what would happen.')

The man inside her head was funny. She approached a bench with irregular steps. She spotted intimate moments between couples. The youthful laughter of a girl erupted from behind a tree and shattered at her feet. The laughter gave her goosebumps as she sat on her solitary bench. Then a formless fear gripped her tight. The lonely afternoon, somewhere far away the faint clamour of cars and urban life, shards of laughter here and there, whispered love, the pestering of peanut sellers and jhal-muri sellers—all of it receded from Lovely, allowing the comfort of the winter sun to take over. If she lay ramrod straight right on this bench, would that be a bizarre sight? If someone looked from afar, all they would see was an ordinary, homely woman in a long, olive-green dress lying on an old wooden bench. Her right braid was almost touching the ground. But what if she lay down and fell into a deep sleep. What if she never woke up, or what if she woke up but fell in love with this park and decided she never wanted to go back home?

Lovely shook off her drowsiness and sat up straight. What nonsense she was thinking!

'Apa, do you want some water?'

It was a young girl, about ten years old, carrying a small enamel jug and a glass. She hadn't felt thirsty, but as soon as she saw the water, her throat felt like parched wood.

'Yes, I do.'

'Five takas a glass.'

'That's fine.'

The girl poured out the water with shaky hands. Lovely emptied the glass at one go and held out the glass to the girl, gesturing for more.

'If you want two glasses, that's going to be ten takas.'

'I know. Just give me another one.'

The girl looked happy. She poured out another glass of water and eagerly held it out to Lovely. As soon as Lovely took the glass, the girl jumped onto the bench.

'Apa, aren't you going to have any lunch? My Ma cooks really good egg polao. All the rickshaw pullers and the CNG drivers around here are her regular customers. She sets up shop at the back gate with her cooking pot.'

'What's your name?'

'Lovely.'

Her answer startled Lovely; her arm shook, spilling the water. The girl looked at her, surprised.

'What did you say?'

'Lovely.'

'How old are you?'

'I don't know.'

'Do you sell water every day?'

'Yes. I have to go now, apa, I have a lot to do.'

The young Lovely ran off. Lovely was still holding the glass. The girl went a few steps ahead, and then bit her tongue before running back to take back her glass. Lovely pulled out fifteen takas from her purse and gave it to her.

'Apa, it's only ten takas.'

'Doesn't matter. Bring me another glass of water in an hour. Will you remember to do that?'

'Yes, I will.'

As soon as the girl left, Lovely began to feel restless. Who knew what the younger Lovely's life was like? She had the same name as her. Did the girl have a sister? Was she called Beauty? *Eish*, she had forgotten to ask. How free the girl looked; she probably roamed the park all day, and ran to her mother for egg polao whenever she felt hungry. Her own life could have been like that! Should she go towards the back gate? She could buy a plate of egg polao and eat, sitting comfortably beside the rickshaw pullers and CNG drivers. Lovely laughed at the thought. The thought of Farida Khanam's face made her laughter grow louder and louder. Her mother didn't tolerate any kind of fraternising with the servant class. She had a very clear notion about her own position. And just imagine her daughter sitting beside a rickshaw puller, guzzling down egg polao!

Lovely's laughter grew until she choked.

('Apumoni, do you have any idea what time it is?')

'I don't. And I don't care.'

('Seriously, Lovely Apa, after all this time, you finally said something after my own heart. But even if you don't want to know, let me tell you. It's now ten past one. Your curfew goes into effect at two. After two, you will be shot on sight.')

'Don't talk rubbish. I turned forty today, forty—do you know what that means? Today I'm going to go back home whenever I want to.'

('Yes, yes, of course.')

The man was hiccupping with laughter again. As soon as she heard the laughter in her head, Lovely wilted. It was true; even if she turned a hundred years old, could she really go back home whenever *she* felt like it? She would probably never be allowed out on her own again—she could guarantee that with her eyes shut.

('Apumoni, listen carefully to what I say. Do you want to go home now?')

'No.'

('Even if you leave right now, you can't be sure that you'll be out of danger. You'll reach home by two, for sure, but it doesn't seem like you'll be able to provide a suitable explanation about what you've been up to all this time. You didn't even get much shopping done. But if you're late getting back, then you're done for—doomed. So what I say is, you're in trouble anyway, whether you're one hour late or three hours. What's the point of worrying so much? You've come out by yourself this one time in your life. Just take in some air, chill, chat with people, then go home. There's no harm if you don't go back at all.')

'What do you mean "chat with people"? Who am I supposed to chat with?'

('Ah, just look to your right. That man who is sitting there in his red and black checkered lungi and cream-coloured tee-shirt, having his ear cleaned—so comfortable that he's dozing off, but still can't stop ogling. I have a feeling he'd be very interested in chatting with you.')

'Apa, would you like some peanuts?' The peanut seller almost whispered right behind her. For a moment, it seemed to Lovely that it was the man inside her head who was asking. When she realised that wasn't the case, she slowly turned around. A young man stood right behind her with a basket of peanuts slung from his neck. Who knew how long he had been standing there. He must have overheard the entire conversation with the man inside her head.

Lovely smiled sweetly at the peanut seller and said, 'Yes, I would.'

'Five takas a pack.'

Did everything cost five takas in this park? The packet was so small that she would have to buy two of them. She was hungry. She had had just one luchi and half an egg that morning, with some vegetable labra, but that had been a while back. All that had been digested a long time ago. Of course, if she went home now, she would get hilsa polao, eggplant cooked in yogurt and spicy duck curry. There would also be a tomato salad, tossed with onions, green chillies and cilantro. To go with the duck meat, there would be brown rice. There was no relief from this menu. Every year, on their birthdays, Farida Khanam prepared this menu with the dedication shown in a religious ritual. Not only that, after the meal, as a *sunnat*, following the Prophet's practice to finish meals with a sweet, there was always rice pudding and homemade sweet curd.

Although a few years ago, on Beauty's birthday, this routine had been broken. There had been no duck. There were no ducks available in the market that day. Not only were there no ducks in Kalmilata Market near their house, Mukhles shaheb had been unable to procure a duck even from Karwan Bazaar. He had returned home with a hangdog expression on his face to deliver the bad news to Farida Khanam.

Overcome with intense grief, as if she had lost someone dear to her, Farida Khanam had to struggle to focus on cooking her daughter's birthday dinner. That year, instead of duck curry, there had been beef bhoona accompanied by rice flour flatbreads. Lovely and Beauty had sat down to the meal with 'disaster has befallen' expressions on their faces, but then, without even realising, they had gorged on the beef bhoona and rutis with great satisfaction. Their father, Mukhles shaheb, had blurted out, 'Farida, the beef bhoona isn't half bad. It tastes quite good with this rice flour ruti.'

'What nonsense. Rice flour ruti and beef bhoona are meant for Eid breakfast. You couldn't find a duck, and I couldn't figure out what to cook, so I just rustled this up. You girls, you don't have to stuff yourselves with beef and ruti just to make me happy. Come, finish off with some hilsa polao.'

--

Lovely was cracking open peanut shells and putting the nuts in her mouth. Every so often, she dabbed a fingertip in the chilli-salt and touched it to her tongue. The thought of having to eat hilsa polao when she got home nauseated her. It would be very unfair to not acknowledge that Farida Khanam was an exceptional cook. Nevertheless, just how long could one go on eating hilsa polao?

Lovely looked around as she ate the peanuts. The man who had been having his ears cleaned was still staring at her, without blinking. The ear cleaner was done with his ears and was now massaging his head. The hard pummelling he was giving the guy's head and neck made an accident seem imminent—he could even break his neck. The man was smiling at her now. Lovely looked away.

'Apa, here's your water. Would you like to eat some fuchka?'

The girl, Lovely, had returned with her second round of water. She wasn't carrying the jug anymore. Instead, three sheuli garlands dangled from her wrist. Lovely finished the water eagerly.

'No, I don't want fuchka.'

'Aren't you going to go home? Where do you live?'

'I don't have a home.'

'Apa, that guy who's standing over there, under that big tree—he wants to talk to you.'

Lovely grew pale. A man was standing under a big tree, and that man wanted to talk to her—what did that mean? Why would he want to talk to her? She stole a glance at the tree and quickly looked away. She couldn't see much. The man was hidden behind the tree. All she could see was his red muffler. It was streaming in the wind, defying the tree's concealment. Lovely realised that the girl was staring at her with intense curiosity. What should she say? There was no way she was going to admit how scared she was. Perhaps her sling bag was their target. If that was the case, there was no need to be scared; she would be happy to hand over her bag. Although she would somehow have to manage to keep the knife. She would probably never have another chance to buy a knife. What was she even thinking, she would *definitely* never get another chance to buy a knife. She had to save the knife. She could unzip her sling bag right now and pull it out. She could stash it under the bench or she could place it on the bench and sit on it. Then, when the man came over, she could hand over her bag with no worry. For him, it would be as if he hadn't even prayed for clouds, but here came some rain.

Lovely noticed that the girl cocked her head and shouted 'coming' before running off towards the man with the red muffler.

('Here's a nice guy who just wants to talk to you, dear Apumoni. So talk to him. Why are you so scared?')

'I don't know him, I have no idea who he is. What can I say to him? Shouldn't I be afraid? What if he's a mugger?'

('Have you ever been out on the streets of Dhaka that you'd run into anyone you know? And have you ever, in your entire life, heard of a mugger introducing himself before mugging someone? Who knows, maybe he just wants to say sweet nothings to you.')

'And my life is so bitter, of course I want to hear sweet nothings from that Red-muffler guy?'

('If we're speaking of bitterness, Apumoni, you have your fair share. There's no point in arguing about that. I'm just having fun imagining what can happen here.')

The girl ran back to Lovely. She was panting from all the back and forth. She gasped as she tried to talk. Instead of three, now there was just one sheuli garland hanging from her wrist. Who knew where the other two had ended up. It hadn't been that long since the girl had left her. She hawked a gob of phlegm right next to Lovely's feet.

'Apa, that guy wants to talk to you. Shall I call him? Look, there he is, in the shade of the tree. You can see him clearly now.'

('Why don't you check him out, Apumoni, see if he looks good?')

What harm was there in looking? She could just turn her head and look at Red-muffler guy. It wasn't evening, it wasn't even late afternoon—it was right in the middle of the day. What could possibly happen? After all, he couldn't slit her throat in front of everyone. If she did feel scared, she could always call out to the head massage guy from the next bench, or even the guy whose head was being massaged. They had both given up any pretense of the massage and were just openly staring at her now. They had probably figured out that something funny was going on. If she even gestured at them, they would fall all over themselves rushing to her. Also, there were many others around, sitting in twos—lovers. The peanut vendor was probably somewhere nearby as well. Lovely mustered her courage and turned her head; she spotted Red-muffler guy right away.

Red-muffler guy had moved a little forward now. He looked respectable but dim. He also seemed much younger than her. Not that being younger than her meant anything; many people were. But why did this Red-muffler guy want to talk to her? Lovely inspected Red-muffler guy more closely this time. He had a timid air about him—Lovely felt her fear dissipate. His smile was uncertain. He was wearing a brown turtleneck sweater, the red muffler, black pants, and his hair was quite long. The wind blew his hair against his face again and again. It made him seem even younger. How old was he? Thirty?

Thirty-two? A thin moustache sat under his nose. Red-muffler guy was glancing this way and that.

('You like him, you like him!')

'Shut up!'

Lovely hadn't noticed when the little girl had disappeared. Surprised, she stared as Red-muffler guy approached her bench step by step. What should she do? Should she stand up and walk away? Should she shout? Should she look away? Lovely was confounded to realise that she was going to do none of those things. Instead, she neatened the hair at her temples, and pulled one of her braids to the front, resting it on her breast. Useless. Red-muffler guy had almost reached the bench in the time it took to arrange herself. When he was close, he stopped again and looked around. What was the guy up to?

Lovely felt a sudden rush inside; she wanted to run away. She would run and run until she was home, and then she would breathe again. Of course, Beauty would be super annoyed. But what would she say when Amma asked her why she was wheezing and so out of breath? For sure, Farida Khanam would get the whole story out of her, bit by bit, like a grater scraping the flesh from a coconut. Then, in the dead of night, Amma would just give her a little tap on the back of her head with a pestle. Game over.

She had absolutely no idea how to talk to an unknown man, or what to say to him. She sat up straight, tidied herself, and waited.

She had been sitting straight for a while now. What was taking him so long? He had almost reached her when she last looked. Just when Lovely had almost decided that Red-muffler guy wasn't coming, just then, right behind her, in fact almost on the back of her neck, she heard a delicate cough. She sat still, powerless to move. Red-muffler guy cleared his throat louder this time. Hopefully, it was Red-muffler guy. What if she turned around now and discovered it was someone else?

'Is there something you'd like to say to me?'

('*Waah*, not a bad start for an amateur, Apumoni!')

Red-muffler guy's coughing ramped up at her question. He coughed so hard, he began flailing trying to control himself. In the soft winter light, Lovely noticed his chapped lips. He swallowed his spit and looked at her in an awkward manner. It was from this moment that Lovely began to enjoy herself. Her disquiet, fear and helplessness disappeared. She flicked her tongue over her lips.

('Say something, Apumoni! Can't you see he's staring at you and gibbering like a fool?')

'Do you want to say something to me?'

'No, I mean, I noticed you were alone, so I came over to talk to you.'

Even this one line was making Red-muffler guy sweat. Carefully, he pulled out a handkerchief from his pocket and mopped his forehead and the back of his neck. The handkerchief was very white. So white that it flamed bright even in the tender light of the sun.

Eish, such a clean handkerchief was now dirtied, thought Lovely. She couldn't figure out how long she should keep her neck swivelled, looking backwards to talk to him. Her neck was hurting already. Oof, how long could she stay like this; if Red-muffler guy really wanted to talk to her he could come and stand in front of her. She noticed that the massage customer was about to fall off his bench from curiosity. Lovely took her time turning back. Behind her, Red-muffler guy coughed lightly a couple of more times and stopped. For a few moments, she heard nothing. It wasn't even clear whether he was still there or not. But suddenly she felt a deep exhalation behind her and immediately, without any warning, a sigh escaped her as well.

Red-muffler guy came and stood in front of her. She had been sitting with her head hung low, so she saw his shoes walk into her line of vision. She looked up quickly and their eyes met.

('Finally! The two pairs of eyes meet! I was about to give up!')

'Can you stop?'

Red-muffler guy said, 'Are you talking to me?'

Lovely paused, then continued in an easy manner: 'No, not you.'

After this strange and unexpected exchange, both went silent.

Red-muffler guy glanced around again. If it wasn't him, who had she been talking to? He felt uncertain.

Lovely felt uncomfortable. What had she just done? She had responded to the man inside her head out loud, that too in front of this stranger. What if this man thought there was something wrong with her? Not only was she ugly but also mental. Who would want to talk to someone like that? If he took to his heels now, could anyone blame him?

'There's this man inside my head who bothers me a lot. I talk to him sometimes. I hope you don't mind.'

The young man smiled shyly, as if he had totally understood the issue with the man inside her head. He mulled over something and, shrugging away his shyness, settled himself in the other corner of Lovely's bench. The lonely middle seat and the peanut packets rested between the two of them.

What was going on with her today? She hadn't even told Beauty about the man inside her head. It wasn't completely true, that she hadn't told Beauty about him at all. She *had* told her, but Beauty hadn't shown any interest. She hadn't asked who the man was, why he was there, how he had gotten inside her head. Not that Lovely could have told her if Beauty had asked—she didn't know any of the answers herself, how could she explain it to Beauty?

But Lovely remembered the exact time—four thirty a.m., the alarm clock ringing ceaselessly like a beggar on a quiet afternoon. Farida Khanam would start banging on the door at any moment. Just as Lovely was telling her sleepy brain to get up because it was time to eat *sehri*, the predawn Ramadan meal, the man inside her head spoke for the first time. ('Apumoni, what's the point in keeping so many fasts? Just pretend you're asleep.')

She had flinched wildly. She had goosebumps all over. She had had no idea who had spoken. She assumed she had been dreaming. Yes, it must have been a dream. She had finally grown certain of the existence of the man inside her head precisely one month and ten days after Riaz's wedding, nine years ago.

'Does the man talk all the time?'

Lovely was taken aback at his question. She withdrew within herself. The whole scene was bizarre, as if none of this was happening to her. This afternoon in the park, eating peanuts, the occasional whisper of a falling leaf, the snatches of conversation and sparks of laughter, and here, this strange young man an arm's length away from her. Lovely pinched herself and blurted out, 'ouch'.

('Apumoni, I'm not quite understanding your deal here. A gentleman is sitting beside you with the best of intentions, and you, instead of chatting him up, are immersed in stupid thoughts.')

'Is the man talking to you right this minute?'

This Red-muffler guy was dangerous! 'No, no, nobody's talking to me. I don't know why I said that. You told that water girl you wanted to tell me something. What is it?'

'Oh, nothing. I was just watching you from over there. You walked over and sat on this bench without looking in any direction. As if you always come here to sit on this bench. I thought maybe you were the reason that I came to this park.'

'Why are you here?' Lovely paused a moment before asking, 'And who do you think I am?'

The young man crumpled. His face turned ashen. This time it seemed like he really did want to run away. He lowered his head and snuck looks this way and that, like a thief. Lovely wouldn't be surprised if he just disappeared right now.

The man inside her head exploded with laughter. It was so sudden that she almost spilled off the bench, like tea from a cup. She was sure that the young man had heard it as well. Because as soon as the laughter started, he turned towards her, startled. Then, he lowered his head again. It didn't seem like he was ever going to look up again, not for the rest of his life. And in that moment, she felt a familiar tenderness for Red-muffler guy. The familiarity frightened her; tenderness led to disaster. Red-muffler guy looked even younger now. He was so uncomfortable even his lips had turned grey.

('Apumoni, this guy is so caught, just look at him.')

'You can say what you want,' Lovely told Red-muffler guy. 'I won't be offended.'

'No, I mean, I've made a terrible mistake. I'm really sorry. I should leave ... please, try to forget about today.'

'What mistake? What should I forget?'

('Didn't I tell you, Apumoni? He's just caught, really caught.')

She shook her head hard. As if she wanted to shake the man out of her head. 'Not another word ...'

'You'll be very hurt if I tell you—I should just go.' The young man strode off in the opposite direction. His red muffler slid off from around his neck at the force of his departure. A desperate lament permeated Lovely. She scrambled off the bench and grabbed the red muffler—how soft and comforting it felt!

('Why are you overthinking it, Apumoni? Call him back, just call him.') The man inside her head also sounded desperate.

'Hey, you, listen, you dropped your muffler.'

The young man stopped and turned around. She stood with the muffler clutched in her hands—her shawl falling away, her long braids and the drooping hem of her kameez pulling her closer to the ground. Did her eyes betray her desperation? Why else did he turn back with such ease? Or had he known that she would summon him with all her mustered hope? Is that why he had dropped the muffler when he stood up? Who knew? She would never know.

Lovely clutched the red muffler tightly in her hands. As if she was never going to let it go. The young man walked back, crossed her, and sat on the bench. She stood there, like a fool, still clasping the red muffler. Then, she too moved towards the bench. She stood close to it, unable to decide whether she should sit down or not. A cold gust of wind shook her to the core. She had never felt herself to be so insubstantial. She grabbed the bench.

A jhal-muri seller had been lurking nearby. As soon as he tried to sidle closer, Red-muffler guy gestured him away with his eyes. The jhal-muri seller left without a single word. For some reason, it seemed to Lovely that he was afraid of Red-muffler guy.

'Sit,' he said.

'I'm going to go home.'

'Where is your home?'

'My home ...'

'It's fine. You don't have to tell me.'

She plopped herself down on the bench and placed the red muffler between them. The knitted fabric lay there, punctuating the space. She lowered her head and wondered why she had just sat down, what this young man wanted from her, what it would feel like to hold his hand and walk around the Ramna Park lake.

Red-muffler guy was barely recognisable now. His awkwardness from before, his trembling lips, his shy glance—it was all gone. Could a person change so swiftly? Or had it all been a sham? All of it a performance strategy for some elaborate theatre. He picked the muffler up in a smooth motion and, folding it messily, dropped it into his lap. Then he threw a brusque question at her, for which she wasn't at all prepared. Even the man inside her head was caught off guard.

'Do you want to come with me?'

'What?'

('What the hell!')

'Do you want to come to my apartment with me? I live alone.' His manner made even this bizarre proposition seem quite normal. As if strangers invited Lovely to their homes all the time and there was nothing in his proposal to make her feel insulted or uncomfortable.

'I have to be home by two.'

Red-muffler guy laughed at her response. The sound of his laughter sliced through the air like lightning. Farther away, someone had brought their children to the park to play in the winter sun. The joyful shouting of the children rolled right up to them. The world transformed to the core; this world seemed very mundane, very plain to her. His laughter swept away her diffidence.

'My mother will be mad at me if I'm late,' she said in a little-girl voice.

'It's way past two already. It's two thirty right now. What does your mother do when she's angry?'

'She sends us to our rooms and locks our doors from the outside. It doesn't bother us anymore. We both have television sets in our rooms. Twenty-inch screens.'

'What do you mean both of you?'

'Me and my sister.'

'How long does she keep you locked up?'

'It depends. Sometimes it's just two or three hours, but sometimes it's like two or three days. Amma opens the door and brings in food, she stays and chats, asks what we want for lunch or dinner. Sometimes she sits and watches television with us, then she locks the door and leaves. At some point, we figure out that our doors are no longer locked, that we can come out of our rooms and everything is fine. We've grown used to it. Today when I get home, she'll probably lock us up for about a month. When Amma locks us, she locks up both of us. Whether it's Beauty's fault or mine, we both get locked up. It's good though; we don't have to do any household chores during those times. We don't have to do the ironing. We just eat, chill out and watch TV. If anyone comes to visit our home when we're locked up, Amma unlocks our doors. We go out normally, and then go back to our rooms when the guests leave. We don't get that many visitors anyway. And anyway, both of us do a lot of skin and hair care during those times. We rub eggs and henna in our hair. And we rub turmeric paste on our arms and legs. It brightens our complexion. Amma has the maid get everything ready for us. Generally, I'm not that into beauty care. I don't enjoy it, and I'm lazy. But when I'm locked up, I do it.'

'It's actually good for you, then.'

'That's true. Those times are also kind of fun. Amma cooks all our favourite dishes. She buys us books. We enjoy those days.'

Blabbing away breathlessly to a complete stranger about the innermost workings of her family's secret punishments gave Lovely a strange sense of peace. For the first time, the young man looked a little perturbed.

He seemed to be floundering among all the things she had just told him.

'Have you never tried to break down the door?'

'Why would we do that? Amma never locks us up without reason. We don't really mind anymore.'

It was clear that Lovely had suddenly thought of something. It made her feel shy, and she even bit down on her tongue. Red-muffler guy noticed the moment; he had never met a woman like her.

'What are you thinking about?' he asked.

'Nothing.'

'Is your father still alive?'

'Yes. His health isn't so good though.'

'Doesn't he say anything when your mother imprisons the two of you?'

'What are you saying? Amma doesn't imprison us. This is why you shouldn't talk to outsiders. I'm telling you one thing and you're turning it into something else. *Arrey*, when we do something wrong, what else can she do? Like, today: I'm supposed to be home by two, and only Allah knows when I'll actually go back. So, you tell me: If she's not going to lock us up for this, what is she supposed to do—coddle us in her lap? That's exactly what Amma says to Abba: If I don't lock them up, what am I supposed to do—coddle them in my lap?'

'What were you thinking about just now?'

'When we're locked in our rooms for three or four days, we go visiting each other, which is a lot of fun.'

'What do you mean you go visiting? Don't you live in the same house?'

'Yes, but we have our own rooms. I call Amma and tell her I want to visit Beauty's house. Oh, I forgot to tell you. My sister's name is Beauty. Then Amma comes to my door and tells me to get dressed. I get ready. Then I tell Amma I'm ready. Then Amma opens the door for me, and we go to Beauty's room. Sometimes it's me and Amma, sometimes it's just me by myself.'

'What do you do when you visit Beauty's house, I mean, her room?'

'We plan, but I can't tell you what the plan is. That's a game Beauty and I play. Although if Amma is visiting as well, we just chat about this and that. We make fun of other people. Beauty's very hospitable and welcoming. She serves me tea and snacks. When she comes to my place, I do the same.'

'How does she serve you tea and snacks? Isn't she locked up?'

'Amma brings it, Beauty serves it. I really like it when we do that. That's also one of our games. Amma enjoys this game too. She never stops us from playing.'

'Doesn't your father play?'

'No, no. This is a game for girls. Abba doesn't play with us. Abba's health isn't so good.'

'Let's go to my place. I too want to play this game with you.'

The man inside her head had been strangely silent. Not a peep out of him. He was lying low. Who knew if he had been rattled by the abrupt turn of events. But now he perked up.

('Apumoni, let's go to his place. It sounds like he will also be quite hospitable and welcoming.')

Lovely strongly opposed his suggestion. She shivered. 'No, no, Amma will kill me if she finds out.'

('How will she ever know? *Arrey*, you're going to have a showdown today anyway. You might as well go all the way.')

She began to answer the man inside her head, but then went quiet. Red-muffler guy was staring at her with the hint of a smile on his lips. Barely half an hour ago, she had thought of this same young man as fearful and timid, someone still wet behind the ears. And now, there was this devious expression playing on his face. A pose, it had all been a pose.

She couldn't decide whether to answer the man inside her head or just go with the Red-muffler guy. It was true that she wanted to follow this young man somewhere. Anywhere. Even if they couldn't go anywhere, they could at least walk along the lakeshore ahead of them. What harm could that do?

'Don't worry about me,' Red-muffler guy said. 'You two go ahead and finish your conversation. I'm in no hurry.'

'I'm not talking to anyone.'

'What's the name of the man inside your head?'

'He has no name.'

'No name?'

'No name.'

'You should give him a name.'

'There's no one inside my head.'

Lovely's eyes teared up. She had no clue where the tears came from or why. She felt like Red-muffler guy was mocking her with the same cruelty that drove children to chase a mad woman with taunts of 'Freak! Freak!'. Children didn't understand how cruel they could be; did he understand?

'Okay, I'm going to go and pick up a couple of cigarettes. In the meantime, the two of you can decide whether you want to come with me or not. No pressure. You only come if it makes you happy.'

The young man stood up, and Lovely immediately became certain that he wasn't coming back. She felt a desperate desire to say, 'Yes, I'll go. I don't have to talk it over with anyone. I'll go.' But inevitably, she didn't. When had her desires ever borne fruit?

Red-muffler guy vanished into the trees of Ramna Park with long strides. The man inside Lovely's head had been burning to talk for a while and couldn't hold himself back any longer.

('You'll never get a chance like this again, Apumoni. How long can you make do with just your fingers? Come on, let's go. What can go wrong? This isn't a guy who's likely to attack you or kill you.')

'How do you know?'

('I know, Apumoni, you're itching to go there. You've never known what love is. Now that you have this one chance, explore it with your heart, with your body.')

'I've never known what love is—how could you say that? My heart still burns.'

('Sorry, Apumoni, I'm sorry. I'm wrong. Of course, you know. But physical love? You'll spend an entire lifetime and then die one day, but you'll never know what physical love is. *What the hell is that?* Just think that the Creator Himself has handed you this one chance.')

'*Tauba, tauba*, shame! No, no. I could never do something like that. You've egged me on to do many shameful things. Amma ...'

('Screw your Amma! Who gives a shit about Amma here? I've egged you on to do many shameful things—is that fair? Was I the one who brought you all that porn by Rashomoy Gupta? All I said was: Put your fingers to good use. But, Apumoni, can buttermilk sate the thirst for cream? That's why I was saying, let's go ...')

'I always knew I shouldn't talk to you. That it would land me in trouble someday, big trouble.'

('Then what's the point in wasting time here? Let's just go home. Amma isn't going to ask you anything today anyway. She's going to feed you well, like a sacrificial cow, send you to your room, and then quietly just lock you in. Then the two of us can take our time figuring out what to tell her.')

'So, what is your name? He was asking.'

('Who's he? Oh, I see. Tell him I have no name.')

'That's what I said. I turned forty today. Forty years old! Imagine that! You're right. I'm going to go with him. I'll clasp his hand and say, take me with you. I want to know, just once, what it feels like.'

('So do I. Although fingers aren't half bad. Apumoni, do you remember that first time? You, the bed, the room—everything just shook and shimmied!')

Yes, Lovely remembered, she remembered all of it. She blushed a deep red in shame, in shyness, in pleasure. *This world made red by red. Oh, mother, your babe has been killed by the killer.*

That day Riaz had shown up at their house around three in the afternoon. Farida Khanam was no longer as delighted as she used to be at his visits. She asked him if he had had lunch in a very unenthused voice. Riaz told her he had. Farida Khanam had asked him the reason for his visit in an even more unenthused voice. Riaz reported, with a guileless expression, that he had come with some study notes for Lovely and Beauty.

The sisters had been prepping for the Intermediate exam as private students. They were officially registered at a college in Kapashia where their maternal grandparents lived; but it was in name only. All they had to do come exam time was to show up at the college and take the tests.

Farida Khanam wanted to see the notes. Riaz pulled out a sheaf of notes for Geography Part II from his bag.

The tight lines on Farida Khanam's face began to slacken when she saw the notes until gradually, they disappeared. She even seemed a little remorseful about her earlier coldness. She had then served Riaz homemade sweet curd with her own hands.

'It's pointless to give those two study notes. They aren't likely to get an education. Useless exercise.'

That day, for the first time in her life, Lovely got her hands on two porn booklets by Rashomoy Gupta alongside the study notes. She devoured every detail in the lines tracing the language of the body. She completely lost control of herself as she read. She couldn't figure out where to hide those books, that treasure hoard.

Lovely hadn't wanted to enjoy that wonder that set her blood on fire, that unfamiliar rapture, all by herself. But as the older sister, how could she place those books in Beauty's hands? Then it occurred to her that Beauty would definitely be able to figure out a safe hiding place for the porn. Riaz's work was efficient; the booklets had been concealed inside the dust jackets of their notebooks.

She peeked into Beauty's room when Farida Khanam went to take her shower. Beauty was focused on removing the polish from her nails. She placed the books on the table in front of Beauty.

'I've already said I'm not going to take the exams. Take these notes and get out of my room. Apa, I told Amma to buy me a VCR. A video-cassette recorder. And she agreed. But after our exams are over.'

'What do you mean buy you a VCR?'

'Buy me a VCR as in buy me a VCR. It'll stay in my room. All of you can come and watch movies here whenever you want to.'

'Why can't it stay in my room?'

'It can't stay in your room because you're not the one who came up with the idea—I did. Anyway, there's another problem with keeping it in your room.'

'What problem?'

'Five weeks out of every four, you're laid up in bed with the lights out because of your headaches. We'll be in trouble then. Watching the latest Hindi movies will be impossible. Instead, we shall be forced to watch Miss Flat on Her Back.'

'I don't want it in my room anyway. But why does Amma buy you whatever you ask for?'

'Amma's afraid of me. When I dig in my heels and argue with her, she gets scared.' Beauty smiled strangely.

'How did you get to be so daring?'

'What do you mean daring? It's a very simple equation. I will obey her, and she will take care of my comforts. Why do you act like a scared mouse all the time, Apa? Listen, inside these walls, we do as we please—do you understand?'

'I do.' Lovely mouthed the words, but it was true that at home she was always timid. Let alone arguing with Farida Khanam, she didn't even have the guts to disagree with her on anything.

She turned around to go, leaving the books on Beauty's desk. Beauty was sitting on the chair with one foot resting on another, her head lowered to focus on her toes. She had talked all this time, almost to herself, without raising her head. As Lovely made to leave, she said without looking up, 'Take these notebooks away, Apa. I told you, I don't need them.'

'They're not notebooks.'

Beauty glanced up at her, but said nothing. That strange smile returned to her lips. Even later, Beauty had never wanted to know where she had gotten those Rashomoy Guptas from, or who had given them to her. Although she did tell Lovely where she had hidden them. She had slid them into a plastic bag and placed them on the overhanging window ledge. She had even slipped in a brick so the bag wouldn't get blown away even during a storm. Their servant boy Harun was in charge of procuring the brick, and he was the one responsible for placing the whole package on the window ledge. Beauty's work was always foolproof.

--

Lovely had made her decision, and as she waited, a multitude of thoughts buzzed inside her brain like flies. Time stopped. There were no sounds anywhere, not even that of falling leaves. The massage-man at the next bench had left ages ago. Even the head massage-recipient had fallen fast asleep on the bench. The silence of the afternoon pressed down on her like death. It seemed to her that this was it, never again would a look of love caress her body. The very pores in her skin grieved. Her dormant feelings pierced her ribs with the force of a doe in heat used as a decoy. Her heart brimming with hunger and despair, Lovely waited.

The red muffler flapped among the trees. The arc of its swing grew wider. The young man looked very thin from this distance. As if he was drifting on the wind, as if he was floating his way back. So he *was* coming back. For the first time in her life, Lovely felt she was a woman. The thought occurred to her that a woman's inexorable attraction had forced a man to return. She had made her decision. She was going with the young man.

As she imagined what could happen between them, her face grew bright red. Or as red as her dirt-coloured skin would allow. Even after forty years, the saga of her dark skin was not done with. Just last night Amma had said, 'Are we going to dump her in the river just because she's *moyla*, just because she's the colour of dirt?' This was directed at Mukhles shaheb. Although Mukhles shaheb barely ever opened his mouth on any issue. Farida Khanam took his silence not as assent, but dissent. Therefore, every hour on the hour, she enumerated all her reasons for not allowing her daughters to be married. This formal delivering of excuses had only been happening for about a month, and its frequency was increasing. Who could have dreamed that Farida Khanam would ever offer anyone any explanation about anything? Was age truly weakening her mind alongside her body? Were the horrors her daughters were destined for in her absence floating right in front of her eyes?

Suddenly a line from a song twirled in Lovely's mind, and in that moment, Red-muffler guy came to stand in front of her. It had to be fate, nothing else, just fate. *Chaltey chaltey yun hi koi mil gaya tha/sar-e-raah chaltey chaltey ... Walking along I met someone/walking along the high road ...*

'Is your consultation over? Let's go. Oh, sorry, I meant, what did you decide? Do you want to come with me?'

('Yes, I do.')

'Yes, I do.'

'It'll be evening by the time you get home ...'

'I know.'

Silent now, she stood up. As she slung her bag on her shoulder, she spotted the peanut vendor. He was standing beside the massive tree to the right, staring at her. As soon as she looked at him, he swung away and walked off. He must have been watching her all this time. The poor guy must have not had much time to spend on his business today. Bengalis were always ready to enter the grave while sticking their noses in the business of others.

Lovely followed as Red-muffler guy led the way. She was feeling really good. If the young man slowed his pace now and clasped her hand, she wouldn't mind even a bit. The song was travelling all across her body right now:

Walking along I met someone/walking along the high road. It was splitting her head in two, and then travelling down to her chest, then down her stomach to her legs, and then back up to her head. What a pain!

For the last year or so, Mukhles shaheb had begun listening to old Hindi movie songs. Singers like Shamshad Begum, Suraiya, Mohammad Rafi reigned in their household these days. In the beginning, the two sisters couldn't stand the music. But gradually, they had grown to truly love those songs; they waited for Mukhles shaheb to put on some Noor Jehan or Geeta Dutt. But who knew they would possess her like this!

'Would you like to eat something?' Red-muffler guy stopped and asked her. As soon as he mentioned food, she felt ravenous. She couldn't recall if she had even finished her five takas worth of peanuts. Hunger was probably why she was getting a headache. Her lips were parched. She licked them.

'No.' There was no certainty in her response.

The scene was thus: Red-muffler guy and she were walking close to the lakeside. There was a path right along the lake. They were strolling along the path; Red-muffler guy walked ahead while Lovely followed. The lake was to their right and to their left were soaring trees. Red-muffler guy had stopped and turned around to ask her the question.

Immediately, their surroundings transformed into a painting. The young man noticed Lovely licking her lips and laughed. He was waiting for Lovely to come closer. When he realised she wasn't going to, he slowly approached her.

'You look like you're super hungry. What's the matter, are you feeling cold?'

She wasn't cold in the slightest; she had just crumbled a little at the young man's proximity. She wrapped her shawl tightly around herself. What was going on, weren't there any other people in Ramna Park anymore? Not a sign of another human being anywhere around them. As if everyone had disappeared in a vanishing act. As if only the two of them had been standing there for an eternity in the park, which was out of this world. A sudden gust of wind shook her to the depths of her soul. She felt numbed by a sudden, deep fear; she felt like she would soil her clothes. Without thinking, she dragged her numb body and began running. She didn't even have the strength to look back. After running for a while, the terror that had emerged so suddenly vanished just as suddenly, and immediately she was drenched in sweat. Farther away, she could see the massive exit—'*Fi amanillah*,' she uttered quietly. 'May Allah protect.'

Now she could see several other visitors in the park. Her courage was crawling back like ants in a line. She stood beneath a tree; she wanted to check if Red-muffler guy would come back this way. She prepared herself for a long wait. She was feeling like a fool for being so terrified despite having the knife in her bag. Her mother didn't call her 'fool of fools' for nothing.

'I was really scared.'

('Me too.')

'Why was I so scared?'

('Apumoni, why are you waiting here?')

'I want to see if Red-muffler guy comes this way. I should go find that girl Lovely.'

('What do you mean?')

'*Arrey*, I'm thirsty.'

('Oh.')

'There he is—there's the red muffler. Give me some advice: should I leave, or should I wait here? You're lecturing me all the time anyway. What should I do? I don't think he'll talk to me anymore. What should I do—should I just leave?'

('I don't know, Apumoni, today your wits seem to be sharper than mine.')

'There are a lot of people around. I can see the road from here. I can hear car horns and see those two three-wheelers right by the gate. What's there to be afraid of?'

It wasn't clear whether she was telling this to the man inside her head or herself. In the meantime, Red-muffler guy had come quite close, although he still hadn't spotted her. He was walking with his head lowered. Lovely softened again; she wanted to slap herself. What sort of stunt had she just pulled! She chatted with the young man, agreed to go to his home, then, like an idiot, just ran away for no reason ... What a tease she was! If Red-muffler guy looked up right now, he would see her. If he didn't look and made a turn, there wouldn't be another chance. She began to pray: 'Allah, grant it, let him look! Allah, grant it, let him look!' And he looked.

Red-muffler guy stared at her in astonishment. He wrinkled his eyebrows, but only for a moment. His forehead cleared, and his gaze alighted on her face like a shard of sunlight from within clouds and then moved away. He was steering clear of her. She lowered her gaze in disappointment.

'Why did you run off like that? If you don't want to go, don't. I wasn't forcing you.' Red-muffler guy had moved a few steps past her before coming back to stand in front of her.

'What time is it?'

'Twenty past five.'

'I want to go home.'

'Come on, I'll drop you off. That's not a problem, is it?'

'It is, but let's go anyway.' She was astounding herself today with her own nerve. An ant grows wings when it's time to die!

'I'm not going to your house today. I can't bring myself to do anything without my sister. Not even if I try a thousand times. I feel bad for Beauty.'

'Okay, maybe another day you can bring Beauty with you.'

Lovely laughed at his response. He had asked her to come another day so easily that she couldn't help laughing at him. This young man didn't have the slightest notion of what their lives were like! In their lives, there was no 'another day'. In their lives, the same day returned again and again, year after year. If, in their lives, a different kind of day appeared, it was like a meteor, manifesting and disappearing.

'Beauty is fairer than I am; you'll like her.'

She didn't know why she said that. She paused for a few seconds before moving towards the exit. Red-muffler guy followed her like a good boy.

('Apumoni, you're going home now for real? This guy here is like a movie star, and you, you just go on and on about Beauty. Beauty doesn't give a hoot about you. How do you think your mother found out about your secret love-games with Riaz? Did you ever ask yourself that? Beauty was the one who ...')

The man inside her head continued to speak, but Lovely didn't want to hear anymore. Before he was done talking, she ran like the devil. Red-muffler guy jolted to a halt where he was, dumbfounded. A commotion arose in the mundane life of the park. A lady, without any warning, had taken off, running all of a sudden. But why, what had happened—the visitors' faces blazed with curiosity about the full story.

For the first time, Red-muffler guy looked truly annoyed. A kooky woman wasn't necessarily a bad thing, but kooky beyond control was trouble.

A bearded man with a skull-cap approached him. 'Bhai, was she a lady pickpocket? You could still catch her if you ran after her right now.'

Red-muffler guy barely threw a glance at him before he too ran like the devil. As if *he* had been the pickpocket and was now being chased by a mob. If he couldn't get away, he had no chance of survival. He ran to the gate and saw that Lovely had already climbed into a three-wheeler. Just as she climbed in, she glanced back and met his eyes. Her eyes were shining with tears. He might have seen wrong. After that sprint, he was panting like a dog with his tongue hanging out, but when he saw her climb into a three-wheeler which was about to leave, he felt something sweep through him. In a flash, he leapt into another three-wheeler and ordered it to follow hers.

Lovely sat quietly as the three-wheeler sped as fast as it could.

('Apumoni, no worries. Mr Red-muffler is right behind us.')

She stuck her head between her knees and covered her head with the shawl. Tears were surging at her like a river. After a long, long time, she enjoyed the freedom of crying like that. She wept.

('Apumoni, what are you doing? Sit up, pull yourself together. Madame General Chief is waiting at home in her black uniform.')

Lovely couldn't hear what the man inside her head was saying. She was remembering how hurt she had been that day. She knew nothing of what had taken place, what Farida Khanam had said to Riaz. Her mother had not said a single word to her. Except one day, like a death sentence, she heard that Riaz would no longer come to their house. She felt as if her ribs had been crushed. Yet Beauty blithely went about her beauty routine as before. She applied egg to her flowing, jet-black hair, and, exuding the odour of egg, she drifted from room to room with no particular purpose. She laughed and joked with Farida Khanam, the two of them falling all over each other, as if they were the best of friends. Yes, Lovely remembered everything.

'Whore! A whore's whorishness never dies. Just wait until I teach that whore a lesson. That devil of a boy, that beast!' Farida Khanam had belched poison with her tongue. For the first time ever, she doubted her own authority and surveillance. Such an enormous transgression had been committed day after day right under her nose and she hadn't had a clue! How dangerous!

Lovely had been locked up for eighteen days after that episode. That was the first time the sisters were imprisoned for something Lovely had done. But Beauty didn't seem upset at all. She was quite happy with her beauty care regimen and watching Hindi movies on the VCR. At times, the joint laughter of mother and daughter floated over from Beauty's room. Farida Khanam would walk by Lovely's room and instruct the maid to cook Beauty's favourite dishes, making sure that Lovely overheard. She would unlock Beauty's door during dinnertime. And one day she even went out and bought a cotton-weave sari for Beauty. At last, one day, the term of imprisonment over, Farida Khanam unlocked Lovely's door. Lovely was sitting quietly, gazing out the window. She turned at the sound of the door and saw Farida Khanam blocking the doorway. Farida Khanam hissed at her in a low voice: 'You don't know me—I'll just finish you off.'

She smiled sweetly in response. Farida Khanam left. Life continued along its rut, just as it had been. A life where the water was calm, without waves. No one in their household ever mentioned Riaz again. Riaz never returned to their house, and even Riaz's mother, their youngest aunt, never came to visit again.

Although 'never' was, perhaps, not the exact truth.

About nine years ago, one day at nine thirty, their aunt did visit with their uncle. Their uncle didn't waste a single word and sat silently the entire time sporting a dour expression. Their aunt, however, did not have a dour expression. A contemptuous smile hung from her lips. They had come to deliver the invitation card to Riaz's wedding. One day, nine years ago.

Their aunt had enumerated all the ways in which Riaz was excelling at his job, and she had praised the foreign bride-to-be with a hundred tongues. Before she left, she had stood in the doorway and told the sisters, 'You two might feel shame that your younger cousin is getting married before either of you. Nevertheless, if you can, do attend.'

Of course, nobody except Farida Khanam had attended. Lovely had really wanted to go, but she was too scared to tell her mother. It was when Farida Khanam was at Riaz's wedding that the two sisters played their dangerous game for the first time. Although Beauty was the one who came up with the idea, it was Lovely who played it to perfection. Exactly one month and ten days after that, the man inside her head had announced his existence.

('Apumoni, what's the point of observing all these fasts day after day? Just pretend you're sleeping.')

--

Lovely couldn't lay low anymore. All this time she had sat unmoving, with her head wedged between her knees. Now, slowly, she sat up. The rush of the wind and the everyday sounds of the road whipped her back to reality. She turned and pushed the three-wheeler curtain aside to try and ascertain if Red-muffler guy really was following her. She couldn't tell. Behind them cars and buses stood in lines, while the three-wheelers flitted through. Her three-wheeler jerked to a stop at a traffic light. The driver had probably wanted to drive through it, but the traffic policeman put a stop to that. The policeman even raised his baton, gesturing as if he was about to hit him.

The three-wheeler driver hissed at the policeman: '*Khankir pola*, you son-of-a-whore, is it your father who feeds me?'

'Listen, I'm right behind you. Are you scared?'

She hadn't even noticed when Red-muffler guy had come to stand beside her three-wheeler. His question made her tremble.

'Just a little. One thing though. I'm going to get out in front of my house, but you shouldn't. Tell your driver to pull on straight ahead. You can see the road from my mother's room; she'll be waiting by the window.'

She had barely finished speaking when the armada of vehicles behind them went mad. The incessant horns and the slivers of swears and slurs that slithered through indicated that the red traffic light had turned green. Red-muffler guy managed to nod before scrambling back to his ride. A bus conductor slapped the side of his bus and spat on the street before teasing, 'Go home! What's all this romancing in the middle of the street?'

Nothing else happened the rest of the way. As soon as she crossed Cooper's Bakery near her house, she began to feel frightened. She began reciting '*Subhanallah*! *Subhanallah*!' to herself. Soon her three-wheeler reached their house and stopped just beyond the metal scissor-gate. Lovely sat inside, taking her time to settle the fare. She wanted to see when Red-muffler guy crossed their house. But there were no three-wheelers behind her. In a while, wearied beyond measure, she climbed out of the three-wheeler with her head drooping. Slowly, she walked to the gate. As soon as she opened the smaller gate nestled within the main gate, another three-wheeler whooshed past.

Lovely felt dizzy. There was something lodged in her throat, threatening to push its way out. Still, with surprising control, she didn't look back. She knew with absolute certainty that Farida Khanam was watching from her window. Even though it was a winter evening, and at six forty her surroundings were blanketed by darkness, Lovely was not willing to risk it.

Without even noticing, she covered her head with her shawl as soon as she walked through the gate. She had missed saying her *Magreb* prayers as well. It pricked inside her; she felt sad. She was going to do her ablutions and perform the missed prayers as soon as she was indoors. She tried to be brave and push away the terror that weighed so heavy in her chest.

With great difficulty, she curbed her impulse to peer at a particular window. She slipped inside the entrance quietly, where another gate stood at the foot of the stairs with a lock hanging from it. She had thought the gate would be unlocked, but it wasn't.

As soon as she pressed the doorbell, she remembered her knife. In a flash, she unzipped her bag, hunting desperately within. She pulled out the plastic-sheathed knife from the bottom of her bag, and, holding her breath, wedged it between her belly and the drawstring knot of her shalwar. Then she wrapped herself well with her orna and her shawl. Her heart was thudding in panic. It had taken less than thirty seconds, but she felt drained. She still hadn't heard the second-floor door open. She inhaled several times before pressing the doorbell again. An inexplicable, uncontainable willfulness spread through her body from inside out. Whatever would happen, would happen. She pressed the doorbell and didn't let up. Had she been pressing it for eternity? She removed her finger from the doorbell when she finally heard the door slam open upstairs.

'Boro Khala, wait there. I'm coming.'

It was that imp. She touched her knife tenderly, as if it was her child.

('Great job, Apumoni! I thought they weren't going to open the door today at all!')

The tiny imp was stomping his way down the stairs while Lovely waited at the base, biting down on her lip.

--

This morning Farida had woken up at least twenty minutes after the time for the *Fazr* prayers was over. This was happening more and more often. Before, she would sit up ramrod straight as soon as she opened her eyes, but these days it took her longer. She told herself the apocalypse wouldn't come just because she opted to stay in bed a little longer.

Even though she had a lot to do today, she was still late getting up. She performed her ablutions and finished her prayers before getting to work. She peeked into the kitchen. Rabeya's Ma, the older maidservant, too, had probably just woken up; sleep still clung to her eyelids.

Farida felt extremely annoyed. She had instructed Rabeya's Ma last night to make whole-wheat rutis for Mukhles shaheb as soon as she woke up. Everyone else would be having luchis today, but his stomach was a little unsettled and wouldn't be able to digest luchis.

'You're as bad as the rest of them. Everyone's a princess in this house.'

'It won't take me a minute to roll out the rutis, Khalamma.'

'Where's that boy? Is that imp still asleep?'

'No, he's up. I saw him go off to sweep the floors.'

'Call him. He needs to go and pick up eggs from the store.'

Rabeya's Ma tried to proffer all the ingredients and equipment needed for luchis to her in a rush.

'Why are you flapping around like a clown? Didn't I just tell you to call that boy? You do exactly what I tell you to, when I tell you to. Don't try to be clever on your own.'

Rabeya's Ma left the kitchen to summon the boy. Farida filled a small saucepan to the brim with water and set it down on the stove. She added oil and salt to the flour in an enamel bowl as she waited for the water to boil.

'Nani, you called me?'

'Go buy some eggs, a dozen. Don't dawdle in the street. Come straight home.'

The boy nodded. Farida untied the knot in her sari-end and handed him some money. Rabeya's Ma had already returned and was quietly preparing the luchis.

'Make the rutis and then make some vegetable labra. Do we have a bottle-gourd?'

'Yes, half of one.'

'Make the labra with gourd, potatoes, cauliflower and eggplant. Call me when it's time to do the tempering. Move it!'

Farida left the kitchen. She would have no peace until every single thing in the house was neat and shiny. She wiped down every object dozens of times a day, every single day. As she crossed her daughters' rooms, she rattled the ring-pulls on their doors as she did every day. 'Lovely, get up, don't miss saying your prayers. Beauty, do your ablutions and say your prayers.'

Farida could tell that Lovely was up already, but Beauty's room was quiet. It would remain that way until nine or ten. The drama would begin once her royal highness woke up. 'Let her—let her do whatever keeps her happy,' she thought to herself. Today she was feeling tenderhearted. Today was Lovely's birthday. Lovely, her eldest. One by one, forty years had gone by. Suddenly her heart grieved for her daughter. She never indulged such emotions. But today there were many things that were out of her control. The thing she usually had the most control over—her heart—had surrendered today. She felt very annoyed with herself.

She entered her bedroom and couldn't remember why she was there. This was another new symptom. She couldn't remember anything; each minute she forgot the preceding one. It often felt as if she had it on the tip of her tongue but couldn't quite get it out.

She sat on her bed for a few moments, hoping she would remember why she was there, but she didn't. She stared unblinkingly at her husband's head that was covered with a blanket. When did he say he was going to visit his village, tomorrow or the day after? He should sort out the division of the land and property as soon as he could. Soon, because of his failing health, he wouldn't be able to make the trip. Even a person like him, without any kith or kin to speak of, apparently had some inheritance. How strange.

'Khalamma, the water's boiling.' Rabeya's Ma's feeble voice from behind the door interrupted her train of thought.

'Okay, I'm coming. Heat some water on the stove for Lovely; she's going to take a bath. Use the big pot and keep half of the hot water for her father.'

Making her way back to the kitchen, she prepared the luchi dough and covered it with a damp dishcloth. She would fry them up hot when everyone sat down to eat. Then she pulled the boti close and started on the vegetables.

'Make sure the rutis are thin. Don't make them thick as if they're meant for labourers. I tell you the same thing every single day, but I see no change.' She was slicing the vegetables, talking nonstop. 'Why are you sniffling around with all that snot? Put your sweater on. Did I give you that sweater for show?'

Rabeya's Ma rolled out the rutis in silence as Farida Khanam talked. She was used to this constant scolding. She no longer let it bother her. The person who treated her own daughters so awfully, didn't treat her too bad in comparison, Rabeya's Ma thought to herself.

'What are you doing, Amma?' Lovely peeked into the kitchen.

'Have you said your prayers yet? Water's heating. Take your bath and then come and have breakfast.'

Lovely nodded. 'What's for breakfast?'

'Luchis, vegetables and eggs.'

Farida returned to slicing vegetables. Lovely stood unmoving by the door, holding on to the door jamb, watching her chop vegetables. Farida suddenly wanted to make her daughter happy. With her usual gruff expression, she told Lovely, 'If you want to go to Gausia, let's do it. See if Beauty wants to go. Her royal highness is still pretending she's asleep.'

Lovely's lifeless eyes gleamed briefly at her mother's proposal, but then dimmed again. Beauty wouldn't agree. And if Beauty couldn't be persuaded, she couldn't go either. Because as soon as breakfast was over, Farida Khanam would settle herself to prepare the routine birthday menu. Then who was she supposed to go with? She dragged her feet as she approached Beauty's door. It was eight twenty-five; it might as well be midnight as far as Beauty was concerned. Lovely didn't hesitate though and began banging on her door. There was no response at all from inside. She lost patience and banged on the door even harder. The noise pulled the just awakened Mukhles shaheb out of his bedroom, his eyes drowsy and fearful. Perhaps he had been afraid that Farida Khanam was already at it with her daughters this early in the day. The fear in his eyes disappeared when he saw it was just Lovely, and he went back to his room. Lovely watched him leave in silence, and then banged on the door again, several times.

'Are you going to break that door down? Go take your bath,' Farida shouted at her from the kitchen. 'Rabeya's Ma, carry the hot water to the bathroom.'

She recalled the moment of Lovely's birth very clearly. They used to live in a three-room tin-roof house near Kamlapur, on Kabi Jasimuddin Road. It was Mukhles shaheb, his still fairly new bride Farida and Mukhles shaheb's sort-of-cousin from the same village, Abdul Bashir. Abdul Bashir had sublet one of their rooms. Mukhles shaheb had just been made a second-class officer at the T&T Board.

Although Bashir shaheb was a diploma engineer by profession, he had started up an export-import business, which was doing quite well. He had to stay in Dhaka quite often for his business, although his wife lived with her parents in Fauzdarhat, Chittagong, with their three children. Bashir shaheb missed his children terribly, but he never mentioned his wife or his in-laws. Neither Mukhles shaheb nor Farida thought much about any of it.

Their only consideration was that they had found a way to supplement their limited income.

Farida felt intensely annoyed at herself for thinking of Bashir shaheb while remembering the moment of Lovely's birth. Her forehead creased into hard lines. The lines didn't disappear for the rest of the day; they grew harsher or eased depending on her annoyance and stress, but they stayed there.

'Khalamma, the rutis are ready. Shall I put them on the table?'

'If you don't put them on the table, what are you going to do with them—stand with them on your head? Are you becoming a bigger fool by the day? Is that bastard boy back with the eggs yet?'

'He is. He's mopping the stairs now. How many eggs should I fry?'

'Fry two now. Make another one when Beauty wakes up. First, go and check whether their father has finished his bath. If he has, tell him to come to the table.'

Just like a ball of yarn that rolled out onto the floor, unravelling farther no matter how you tried to chase it down, the moment she thought of Abdul Bashir, memory after memory unwound in her mind, making her lose her composure. No, there was no way she would allow this clutter of thoughts to ruin today.

Farida almost shoved Rabeya's Ma aside and left the kitchen. She began shouting for everyone to gather at the breakfast table.

'Lovely, come quick. Everything's getting cold. I'll fry the luchis once you all sit down so they're hot. Is Beauty up yet? Hey, Beauty, hey, get up! Is she even listening? All of them, deaf! You devil, come and finish breakfast so I can get some relief!' She banged on Beauty's door. Not that it worked. Beauty wasn't likely to get up so easily. Farida rushed back to her bedroom, perhaps to check whether her husband had bathed yet.

Mukhles shaheb was out of the bathroom and had just settled himself on his prayer mat. Farida began to talk as soon as she entered, but when she saw Mukhles shaheb praying, she swallowed her words. But she couldn't suppress her agitation. She went to the window and drew the curtains. Outside, Monipuripara was still sleepy and slothful. As she stared at the somnolent alley, she prayed '*Ya nafsi*' to herself under her breath. Suddenly, as something occurred to her, she swept out of the room again.

Breakfast was on the table. Rabeya's Ma was filling water glasses.

'Rabeya's Ma, get the duck out of the freezer. Thaw it in lukewarm water.'

Farida no longer took any risks with buying the duck. She bought the duck a month early and stuck it in the freezer. She had been doing this for the last two years to circumvent any possibility of 'couldn't find one at this last minute'. Although she didn't approve of frozen duck. But what choice did she have! Even a frozen bird was better than none. Every breath she drew was dedicated to ensuring that everything worked as perfectly, as consistently, as the laws of nature. The point to be noted was that nothing was working perfectly. Farida was well aware of this. So, her efforts and persistence were moving beyond reasonable day by day.

--

Lovely emerged from the shower. She hadn't dried her hair very well; she was dripping water. She went to her room. If she didn't dry her hair properly, she would catch a cold. She couldn't bear to cut her long hair, but it was a pain to dry. The other day, while she was asleep, Beauty had almost chopped it off. Rabeya's Ma had brought a cup of tea to Lovely's room and spotted Beauty hunched near her head wielding a pair of scissors. She screamed, immediately waking up Lovely.

Lovely's scrambling to sit up at being woken so abruptly was nothing compared to Beauty's scrambling to get away from her. She was so startled that she cut her own hand, resulting in more drama.

Farida Khanam had almost dismissed Rabeya's Ma that day. The woman had strict instructions never to enter the girls' rooms unbidden. She was only supposed to go to their rooms when she was told. But she paid no attention to that. She visited Lovely's room or Beauty's room at any chance she got. She only got to keep her job because Farida Khanam had softened these days, both in mind and body. Four or five years ago, Rabeya's Ma would have been sacked straightaway. Finding a good servant these days was as impossible as having the moon in your hand. Also, Rabeya's Ma had another thing going for her. She had no family anywhere. Her only child, her daughter Rabeya, had died in childhood; Rabeya's Ma couldn't even say for sure when or on what day. She didn't talk too much; she didn't talk back even if yelled at a thousand times. All she wanted was to watch television sometimes. Farida Khanam didn't refuse her that. After all, they were human too!

Lovely towelled her hair and then dried it some more with a hair dryer. She'd be in trouble if the noise reached Beauty, who had become an authority on beauty practices. She had read in some magazine that blow-drying damaged hair, so now not only did she not use the hair dryer herself, she wouldn't let Lovely use it either. Although Beauty was the one who had made Farida Khanam take her to Eastern Plaza to buy the thing. It was funny, but every modern luxury item that she used had once been owned by Beauty. Once Beauty grew tired of them, they were handed down to Lovely.

For instance, there was a tiny CD player in her room. Which, obviously, had once belonged to Beauty. After using it for a few days, Beauty had brought it over to her room one afternoon. 'Apa, you keep this CD player.'

'What will I do with it?'

'What do you mean what will you do with it, you'll listen to music. Why do you talk like an idiot?'

'But I can go to your room to listen to music.'

'You can still do that. I told Amma to get me a new one.'

'Why, what's wrong with this one?'

'Nothing's wrong with it, it's just old. The sound is so feeble. Sound has a major role to play in how we experience music.'

Of course, getting that CD player was a blessing. She could listen to music whenever she wanted, at a low volume. She no longer had to depend on Beauty's moods.

--

Mukhles shaheb approached the breakfast table when he was done with his prayers. These days he felt a crazy hunger as soon as he woke up. He felt a little helpless. Neither mother, nor daughters were anywhere to be seen. He harboured a sliver of suspicion about whether Farida Khanam would actually allow him to eat any luchis. He couldn't see any luchis on the table, but they must have been prepared; after all, today was Lovely's birthday.

'Why are you sitting with your hands folded? Eat.'

'What about Lovely?'

'She'll eat too, why wouldn't she? Lovely, aren't you done with your bath yet?'

Lovely entered the dining room and took her seat.

'Rabeya's Ma, fry up the luchis.'

Lovely and Mukhles shaheb both looked at Farida Khanam. The process of frying up the luchis was entirely Farida Khanam's own thing. It was unthinkable that she would allow anyone else to be part of that. Although, four months ago, when it was Beauty's birthday, Lovely had been tasked with stirring the birthday rice pudding. So sometimes even the inexorable laws of nature were subject to change.

——

Farida herself felt a little taken aback at her own order to Rabeya's Ma to fry the luchis. It was becoming very clear day by day that both her mind and her strength were waning.

'Tempering those vegetables tired me out. Both of you, go ahead, start. Rabeya's Ma, make sure the luchis puff up properly.' She turned to her husband. 'The kitchen fan needs to be replaced. It doesn't spin. I should call in a repairman to check it first. Although it can wait until winter's gone.'

'I don't think it can be repaired; it's at least ten or twelve years old.'

'If it can't be repaired, it can be replaced. There's no harm in getting someone to look at it first.'

'That's true.' Mukhles shaheb went silent. He didn't want to annoy Farida and ruin any prospect of luchis.

The servant boy brought in a plate with a couple of luchis. Farida inspected the luchis intently before placing one on Lovely's plate. She was a little disappointed. They had puffed up quite nicely.

'Farida, today is a special day. It won't do any harm if I have a couple of luchis.'

'Who told you it won't do any harm? Are you a doctor?'

'Amma, let him eat just one.'

'Now you're showing all this love for your father, but I'm the one who will have to take care of him if he gets sick. Okay, fine, go ahead and take one.'

Farida felt satisfied. Even if her mind and her strength were about to go, she was still the mistress of this household—she had the final word. She fed her husband and daughter with the utmost tenderness. No matter what they were like, he was her own husband, she, her own daughter!

When Farida had left the bustling home of her parents in the village to build her own family and household with her husband, she wasn't sad at all. She hadn't been one of those girls who were mad about weddings; neither was she the kind who played with dolls from the age of ten, as proxies for their own children and households. But her tie to what was hers, her blind devotion to what belonged to her, had always superseded everything else. *My* house, *my* siblings, *my* parents—this concept of *mine* was dangerously alive in her. What could be more 'mine' than her own husband and her own household? The day she first set foot in her husband's house, 'my husband' and 'my household' easily became closer to her than 'my father's home' or 'my brothers and sisters'. Everything else could be cast aside when compared to husband and home.

The other thing that was remarkable about Farida was her dedication to perfection. Everything she did *had* to be perfect. Many marriage proposals had arrived for her daughters. But in the end, she couldn't bear to give either of them away to any of those grooms. Every prospective groom had some blemish; none were perfect. Was she supposed to give her daughters away to whoever came by, as if she was tossing them into the river? Such thinking doomed all marriage prospects in the end. Although her heart felt a little uncertain these days.

Lovely returned to report that Beauty was still asleep. Farida was incensed. 'What is this! No regard for the time of day or anything! Every single God-given day she stays in that room until noon. It's your sister's birthday today, so at least make the effort to get up early! That devil ... that devil is due for some harsh punishment!'

Farida furrowed her eyebrows as she cursed. She instructed Lovely to get ready. She was still hoping that if she banged on the door a few more times, Beauty would emerge.

It took Lovely barely ten minutes to get ready. Farida's heart wept when she looked at her daughter's face. Age had left its mark on her. When had this happened? Since when had this girl started becoming an old woman? As soon as she felt her eyes tearing up, she hardened her expression. She pummelled Beauty's door. Not only did Beauty not open up, there wasn't the slightest response from inside. She felt tired. The realisation that she would have to drag this household along from dawn till dusk numbed her.

She could refuse her daughter now. She could tell Lovely, since Beauty's not opening her door, don't go out today. Or she could tell her to wait for Beauty, which meant it would be past noon before they could leave. What was the point in going then? They wouldn't be able to make it back by lunchtime. Or she could get herself ready in a couple of minutes and go out with Lovely.

Farida got up thinking that was the only solution. But if she went out, who would do the cooking? Duck curry and hilsa polao. No, there was no way she could go. She walked into her bedroom and then out again as she worked through her thoughts. There was nothing to be done; Lovely would just have to go out tomorrow, or the day after. The three of them could go together, or perhaps it could be just the two sisters.

When she exited the bedroom, she saw Lovely at the dining table with a cup of tea in front of her, her black bag hanging from her shoulder. Her long braids dangled helplessly on either side. She wasn't sipping her tea; she was merely tinkling the spoon against the cup in a preoccupied manner. Her posture was clearly of someone awaiting a verdict. She wouldn't sulk, she wouldn't protest; she would silently accept whatever was doled out to her.

'Go on, don't delay any longer. Be home before lunchtime. Choose one, or maybe two, shalwar kameez sets for yourself. Buy one for Beauty as well. Or, no, there's no need for that. Let that *haramjadi* sleep.' She startled herself with what she had just said. She had just told Lovely to go out by herself. What the hell was she doing?

'Amma, should I go by myself?' Lovely sounded incredibly helpless. As if she had just been instructed to navigate an ocean on her own.

'If not by yourself, are you going to go out with a police escort? You say such pointless things all the time.'

Lovely still couldn't quite believe it. Amma would probably say any moment, 'Just wait, I'll show you! Going to Gausia by yourself! How dare you!' But Farida Khanam said nothing. She went off to the kitchen, and began berating Rabeya's Ma over something. Not a single word entered Lovely's ears, but she couldn't quite work up the nerve to leave by herself. Could a habit formed over forty years be overturned by a single word? Not even by a word from Farida Khanam.

'Why are you sitting there like an idiot? Didn't I tell you to go out? Take a CNG three-wheeler. Pay him whatever he asks. Don't argue about the fare. How much did your father give you last night, twelve hundred or two thousand?'

'Two thousand.'

——

As soon as Lovely stepped foot outside, fear and uncertainty bit down on Farida's heart. She felt parched inside, from her tongue to her vocal cords. She wanted to shout with all her might: 'Where are you off to by yourself? You *haramjadi*, how dare you! Don't you know me yet? I'll break your limbs!' But not a single word emerged from her mouth. The front door swung shut slowly, right in front of her eyes. She barely made it to her bedroom window. The window overlooked the entrance to their alleyway and the road beyond. She waited with bated breath; she spotted Lovely within a few seconds.

Lovely opened the small gate nestled in the belly of the larger gate and walked out. She covered her head with her orna and wrapped her shawl tightly around herself. Farida hoped that Lovely would look back, towards her window. Then she could tell her to go quickly or something like that, but Lovely never looked back, not once. She stood outside the open gate, as if she wasn't sure about what to do. Farida called at the top of her lungs: 'Hey, boy! Are all of you dead?'

'Yes, Nani?'

'Go, quickly. Lovely is waiting by the gate. She's going to Gausia. Go and get her a CNG three-wheeler.'

'Boro Khala's going by herself?' The boy, during his two and a half years of employment, had not seen either of the two khalas go anywhere by themselves, and was slightly perturbed.

'All you do is talk. I feel like knocking your teeth out. She must have reached the mouth of the alley by now. Run! Come back as soon as you've got her a CNG, do you understand?'

He barely nodded before sprinting off. That very moment, a sense of dread permeated Farida's heart. She had no doubt that she had just made the biggest mistake of her entire life. Even on this winter morning, she turned the ceiling fan on at full speed, and sat down on the bed. For a moment, she thought she might as well head for Gausia too. But she couldn't muster the strength to get up, open the door and go out. A thought occurred to her for the first time: neither Mukhles shaheb nor she were young anymore—how long would they live? What would happen to the girls then? They would have to make their way in the world on their own. Right, it was a good thing to have sent Lovely off by herself today. Let her get used to it. But even these thoughts didn't calm her down. Her limbs were growing ice-cold.

'Khalamma, the duck has thawed. I made a paste of ginger and garlic.'

Farida Khanam barely heard Rabeya's Ma. Or perhaps Rabeya's Ma had spoken loudly enough, but she didn't hear her because she was submerged so deep in her own thoughts. 'What?'

'The duck's thawed.'

'Speak properly. Why are you mewling like a new bride? Did you make the ginger-garlic paste?'

'Yes, I did.'

'Turn the fan off. Go tidy up Lovely's bed. *Arrey*, why are you running off before I'm done talking? Is the boy back yet?'

'I didn't see him.'

'Go and check whether he's back. If he is, send him to me right now.'

The boy came and stood outside her door. The door-curtains swished at his touch.

'Nani, you called me?'

'Didn't I tell you to come home as soon as you got her a CNG? Don't my words reach your ears?'

'I did come back as soon as I got her a three-wheeler.'

'Did she get in all right?'

'Yes, she did.'

'Was the driver young or old?'

'He wasn't very young—like, kind of old.'

'Are your morning chores done?'

'Yes. Nana is asking for the newspaper.'

'Why are you telling me? Am I waiting around here with the paper? Go and get it from the living room. Where is he?'

'He's sitting in the back veranda.'

--

If only she had had an existence as untroubled as Mukhles shaheb's. He was neither right, nor left, nor ahead, nor behind. He was nowhere really. He was skimming his way across an almost non-existent, anesthetized life.

When Farida returned to her father's house a few days after their wedding on her *naiyor* visit, she herself spent her first few days similarly benumbed. Farida's mother had been a formidable woman. Their enormous household operated completely under her thumb. Even Farida's paternal grandmother heeded her every word. She was a tiny woman, but in her movements and appearance, she was like a lioness. People said that everything she touched turned to gold. Farida's grandmother bragged about her blessed daughter-in-law to everyone. Even beggars visiting their household had to listen to the stories.

'Isn't there anyone who can bring this beggar a fistful of rice? She's been waiting here for ages!' her grandmother would call out before continuing, 'So, you know, the very day that my middle daughter-in-law stepped foot in this household, the story changed. Our fortunes jumped from here to here in the blink of an eye.' To show how big a jump it had been, Farida's grandmother would lay her palm flat close to the ground and then swing it up to her shoulder. Her eyes radiated joy. Perhaps Farida's mother would be walking past then, or perhaps she would be sitting in the yard, massaging oil into the hair of Farida and her siblings. Her mother-in-law's praise did not please her.

'Amma, will you stop!' she would say. 'Why do you need to chat so much with strangers!'

Even that scolding brought great joy to Farida's grandmother. The listeners' eyes would startle as they watched the blessed daughter-in-law behave so rudely with the mother-in-law.

On the second day of her *naiyor* visit, Farida's mother called her in for a private chat. Farida and her four siblings were terrified of their mother; but their father was as easy as milk and rice. If Farida's mother asked about something, the ironclad rule was that she *had* to be answered truthfully. Even Farida's grandmother never veered from that commandment.

'You're visiting your father's house after your wedding. Why are you so glum? What's wrong?'

'There's nothing wrong, Amma.'

'Of course, there is. The question is whether you want to talk about it or not.'

Farida sat quietly for a very long time with her head lowered. Amma didn't hurry or nudge her during that long silence. She sat embroidering flowers on a pillowcase.

'I don't want to talk about it.'

'If you don't want to talk about it, you shouldn't. But I think it would be good if you did. I could think up a solution.'

'There is no solution.'

This time, Farida's mother was quiet for a very long time. Finally, she jabbed the needle into the pillowcase and set it aside in a leisurely manner. A thin line of anxiety barely creased her forehead like a crescent moon before disappearing again.

'After Rahela's marriage, I took so much time and made such an effort to arrange your wedding. I can't bear to see the way Rahela endures the torture at the house of her in-laws. I thought I'd made a terrible mistake marrying my eldest daughter into such a large family. I wasn't going to make the same mistake with my younger daughter. I married you to a man who had no one to call his own in the world. Your groom is a golden boy in every possible way. He has a good job, he's good-looking, and he is polite and respectful. Farida, look at me!'

Farida's head hung even lower. At that moment, she had just wanted to disappear into the ground. Nineteen was quite old for marriage back in those days. Perhaps it had taken so long because they had been searching for a man who had no kin in the world.

'Farida, look at me! I don't like repeating myself.'

Farida managed to look up and blurt it out: 'He had told Bhai Jan very clearly that he didn't want to get married.' She couldn't look at her mother for too long. Her gaze lurched about like a slaughtered chicken.

'People talk nonsense when they're young. Your husband and our Akbar were classmates. He just felt shy about the proposal to marry his friend's younger sister. That's all there was to it. Why are you making such a big deal out of this, what's the problem?'

'He is not capable of being a husband.'

Farida murmured this so quietly that her words almost disappeared into the air. The concern creasing her mother's brow now descended to her eyes. For the first and last time in their lives, she weakened in front of Farida. She grabbed hold of the enormous bed with both hands and, opening her mouth wide, gasped. Even after seeing her mother like that, Farida did nothing. She stood where she was and didn't budge an inch. Neither mother nor daughter knew how much time passed. But after a long while, the mother pretended to gather herself. It took some effort, but eventually she let go of the bed and sat up straight. This time she consciously avoided her daughter's gaze. She cleared her throat.

'Not a bird or a bug should ever find out. The duty of a worthy woman is to absorb. That is what you will do. Whatever has happened is fate. Don't let people laugh at you—never give them the chance to laugh at you. Your husband's humiliation is your own. Now, that house is your own, that man is your husband—no matter what he's like.'

Every word her mother uttered hammered into Farida's brain. Of course, she had known that she would have to endure the marriage, that now it was her job to uphold her own honour. In all her life, Farida had but one regret: she should not have spilled the innermost workings of her own household to her mother. She had no other regrets.

After that conversation, Farida didn't stay much longer at her father's house. Four days later, she almost forced her way back to the town where her husband worked. Her cousins pursed their lips and sniggered. Her utter devotion to her husband's house in just the few days that she'd been married gave rise to endless snide comments and mockery. Farida dealt with it all: sometimes with pretend-anger, sometimes with a shy smile. But she departed from her father's house with a blissful expression. Mukhles shaheb was astounded.

Farida said her farewells to her father, her older brother, her eldest uncle and his wife by touching their feet. She touched her mother's feet after she had paid her respects to everyone else. Her mother stood before Mukhles shaheb, and told him directly, '*Dula Mia*, Farida is my daughter. My daughters are worthy; always remember that.'

No one understood why Farida's mother would say such a thing. And so, no one had anything good to say about the mother-in-law's arrogance. In fact, for the first time in their lives, even Farida's father expressed dissatisfaction with his wife. He told her this, with some trepidation, after their daughter and son-in-law had left. Farida's mother, for the first time in their lives, admitted her fault; but she did not reveal the secret.

As Farida and her husband were about to leave, her mother called her to her room. Farida was covered in jewellery: a dozen bangles on her wrists, anklets on her feet. She entered her mother's room as if accompanied by an orchestra. Every time she moved, she tinkled and jangled. She was looking very comely. The mother gazed at the daughter in loving rapture for a minute.

'I am very pleased, my child, very pleased. You are a true daughter of mine.'

Farida stood smiling in front of her mother, her head held high. She held her head so high that soon her neck stretched and stretched like a giraffe's. The head that she raised that day never came down.

'Khalamma, I've soaked the laundry. Give me some detergent.'

Farida hadn't noticed when Rabeya's Ma had quietly entered the room. The rule for servants was that they should make some sort of noise at the door to announce their presence, then Farida would ask what they needed, and only then could they enter the room or speak from the doorway. But it was impossible to get this through to Rabeya's Ma, even though she had worked in the house for six years.

'Haven't I told you not to enter my room unannounced? It doesn't seem to register in your brain.'

'I waited in the doorway and called to you twice, Khalamma.'

'What do you mean "I called to you"? Did I give you permission to enter the room?'

Rabeya's Ma didn't really have an answer to that, so she just shut up like usual. Farida felt suspicious. Had she really been sunk so deep in her thoughts that she hadn't heard Rabeya's Ma call, twice? Now she couldn't remember why Rabeya's Ma had come to her. She felt defeated. 'What do you want?'

'I need detergent. I soaked the laundry.'

'Go to the bathroom, I'll bring it over.'

This was another of her habits—to keep rice, potatoes, onions, cooking oil and laundry detergent under lock and key. She acted as if allowing the servants unlimited access to these supplies would soon render her family destitute. The amount that would last a month if she doled it out herself would barely last them two weeks if the servants were allowed direct access. This theory had never actually been tested; however, her belief was unshakeable.

'Rabeya's Ma, come back here.'

Rabeya's Ma returned.

'Is Beauty up yet? Has she had any breakfast or is she still asleep?'

'She's up. She's put egg in her hair and told me to heat some water for her bath. She wants to have breakfast after she bathes.'

The mobile phone rang. There was no landline in this household, there never had been. It took quite a long time, even after cellphones became commonplace, for a phone to find entry into this house. The phone rested on Farida's dressing table, hooked to the charger at all hours. It was rare for someone to call this house; rarer still for someone from this house to call outside. Farida jumped up like a coiled spring. Who was it—was it Lovely? She must be calling from a store or somewhere else for some reason. Although Farida strongly doubted whether Lovely knew their number by heart. She should have written down the number for Lovely before she left. She was slipping up so badly these days, she couldn't even trust herself anymore.

'Hello? Who is it?'

'Is that Farida? It's me.'

'Me? Who's me?'

'Abdul Bashir.'

Farida froze like a winter's night. Her forehead sliced into creases. Before she could decide whether to respond or just hang up, Abdul Bashir grew impatient on the other end.

'Did we get disconnected? Hello, hello, Farida ...?'

'Where did you get this number?'

'That's a long story. Forget about that. How are you all? Lovely? Beauty?'

'Haven't you been told never to call this house? How dare you?'

Farida didn't notice that her voice had dropped several registers and she was hissing at him like a snake. What if Lovely or Beauty had picked up the phone? This man was so evil, who knew what he would have told them! Even the possibility of that imagined conversation gave her goosebumps. She felt as if the blood was leaving her body and her legs were turning to mush.

'I've been thinking, Farida. You've terrorised me all this time, and I have been terrified for no reason. I'm old. We're all old. We're not rookies anymore.'

'What do you want?'

'I want to see Lovely and Beauty.'

'Impossible. I wasn't scaring you. I was telling you the truth. If your wife and your children ever find out, will they allow you to stay with them any longer?'

'So you haven't heard the news. My wife Khodeza passed away about two months ago. It's no use bringing all that up, Farida. I don't care anymore.'

'I'm telling you this very clearly. If you make any attempt to contact my daughters, I will burn everything down.'

'You can't burn anything down. If you try to set fire to anything, you'll be the first one to burn. The one person for whom I kept my mouth shut all these years is now gone, so ...'

Farida hung up. Her insides were flopping about like a stranded fish. She clenched the phone in her fist, as if it was Abdul Bashir's throat. For a long time, or perhaps for just a few moments, Farida remained motionless, her thoughts roaming the earth and the sky. She tried to control herself. The hardness of her expression and her consternation lessened somewhat. She turned the phone off and put it back in its usual place. Then she exited the room with her usual air of authority.

——

In the kitchen, Rabeya's Ma was slurping tea. When she saw Farida, she stood to attention like a soldier. But she couldn't figure out where to put down her teacup.

'I left the detergent in the bathroom. Call me when you've finished the laundry. Where's that *haramjada*—

that bastard boy? There's been no sign of him since morning.'

'He's plucking Khalu Jan's grey hair. Should I call him?'

'No, no need. When he came back, did he lock the door downstairs? Where's the key? Oh, forget it, I'll go and check whether he locked it or not.'

She exited the kitchen as if she had been chased out of there. Somehow, she managed to open the front door and dart down the stairs. The set of steps to the second floor and the set of steps to the roof had been separated with an iron grille from which hung an enormous padlock. She pulled at it for no good reason; it was clearly locked. She stood on the staircase and stared like a hawk at the two apartments on the other side, as if someone from one of them was spying on them. Although one of those flats was empty. The tenant had left just last month. They hadn't even put up the 'To-Let' sign outside the building yet. The other apartment was occupied though. The tenants were a middle-aged couple. Their only son was studying somewhere abroad, who knew where; Farida had never asked. She did not approve of being over-friendly with tenants. Earlier, the first-floor apartment had been just like theirs. Later, after thinking it over, she had another kitchen built and split it into two apartments. Now the combined rent amounted to quite a bit of income for them.

Farida tugged at the lock to reassure herself before climbing back upstairs. No, from now on, she was going to take the key that the boy usually had and keep it with herself. He just had to ask her for it when he went out. Why hadn't she thought of this before? Of course, the boy didn't have the key when Farida wasn't home; it was with Mukhles shaheb on those occasions. When she was home, she let the boy keep the key only during the daytime because she needed to send him out on various errands a hundred times a day. But he handed the key back to her before evening descended.

Farida decided she couldn't allow that anymore. Otherwise, one day she would find Abdul Bashir sitting in her living room, sipping tea with salted biscuits. Something like that had happened last week. The boy ran off with the keys the second the doorbell rang. *Arrey*, first check to see who it is—but the imp disappeared before she could say anything. That day it had just been the vegetable-vendor. But it could very well have been Bashir instead of the vegetable-seller. The thought made her heart stop.

She felt exhausted as she climbed the stairs. The door to their apartment stood open; the dining room was to the right as one entered, the living room to the left. The living room door was mostly kept shut. Every morning, along with all the other rooms, the boy swept and mopped the living room. He dusted everything and then fastened the door. The kitchen was adjacent to the dining room.

Farida entered the dining room and saw Beauty at the table, eating breakfast with a towel wrapped around her head. She became aware of the faint odour of eggs as soon as she stepped into the dining room. Beauty was engrossed in her luchi and eggs and paid her no attention. The sight of her sent Farida's temper through the roof.

'Lovely, me—we almost broke down your door this morning, and not a peep from you. That's how horrible you are!'

Beauty didn't seem the least bit perturbed. 'Why are the luchis like this? They're like limp rags.'

'Her royal highness has deigned to show up for breakfast at eleven, and thinks the luchis are like rags. Rabeya's Ma fried them. Do you want me to fry a couple for you?'

'Yes. Where's Apa?'

'She went to Gausia.'

'To Gausia? How?'

Beauty forgot to chew as she uttered the question. Her jaw dropped and she stared at her mother. Farida turned away from her slack-jawed face and walked to the kitchen. She didn't feel like answering Beauty's question just then. And anyway, Farida Khanam did not owe anyone any explanations.

Beauty replaced the piece of luchi on her plate instead of putting it in her mouth, and followed her mother into the kitchen. Farida Khanam picked up a rolled out luchi from underneath the damp towel where they rested, and waited in front of the frying pan full of oil. She would toss the luchi in once the oil was properly hot. Rabeya's Ma wasn't there. She must have been washing the clothes.

'Did the boy go with Apa?'

'Why would the boy go with Apa? Doesn't he have chores to do here?'

'Then who did Apa go with? With Abba?'

'No, she didn't go with anyone. She went by herself.'

'By *herself*?'

Beauty had never heard such an astonishing thing in her life. She was livid. She had never had the chance to go anywhere by herself; it wasn't even an option. And here was Apa, blithely traipsing off to Gausia, and not even secretly—Amma herself had sent her. Her blood boiled at witnessing such gross injustice right in front of her eyes. Farida Khanam had always had two different sets of rules and judgements for the two of them.

'Have you ever let me go anywhere by myself? Why did you let *her* go? I'm also going to Gausia right now.'

'Just try it. As if I wanted to let her go by herself. Our fists were sore from banging on your door. You're shameless, talking back at me now. A slap is what you'll get. Go back to the table; I'll bring the luchis.'

'Tell me when you'll let me go. Tell me!'

'Let you go where?'

'What do I know, where? Tell me when you'll let me go out by myself!'

'You don't even know where you want to go. You just blather nonsense all day long. You do no work at all, you're a big girl just sitting on your ass—aren't you ashamed of yourself? Get out of my sight!'

'Amma, I'm telling you. Tomorrow I'm going out by myself. Don't try to foist Apa on me.' Beauty's voice was icy.

Farida was afraid of this side of Beauty. She never disobeyed her mother, but Farida knew very well that she could easily do so if she wanted to. Lovely wasn't capable of that.

'Beauty, I'm telling you, just finish your breakfast.'

'I'm not hungry. Why don't you go and feed this breakfast to your beloved eldest daughter?'

'How dare you! Your days are numbered, just you remember that.'

Beauty wasted no more words. She went straight to her room. She was going to prop herself comfortably on her bed and watch *Jodha Akbar*. She was feeling quite smug; she had given her mother quite the tongue-lashing. But what astounded her was Lovely's nerve. She had gone off by herself just because Farida had told her to ...? If Beauty had been told to do the same, the cat would have been out of the bag. No matter what big claims she made when shooting off her mouth, she doubted that she would have had the guts to pull that off. It was no joke. It was a huge, big deal for someone who had never ever gone anywhere by herself before. She felt a smidgen of respect for her elder sister.

Beauty laughed as she thought about capitalising on this chance of squeezing something good out of their mother because she had let Apa go out by herself. She brooded over what she could get out of Amma, which reminded her of the time she got the VCR. The day Beauty had asked for the VCR, Farida Khanam had fallen from the sky in surprise.

It had been four thirty in the afternoon, or maybe five. Time for afternoon tea. Beauty had gone and stood outside Farida Khanam's room with a grim expression. 'Amma, can I come in?'

'Why, what do you need?'

'Can I come in or not?'

'Cut out the drama. Come in.'

Beauty entered Farida Khanam's room. She didn't bother with small talk. She demanded directly: 'Amma, buy me a VCR.'

'Buy you what?'

'A VCR.'

Farida Khanam usually took a nap after lunch. She didn't exactly sleep, but she lay down for a while with her eyes closed. That afternoon, she had still been dozing. She was still a little drowsy when Beauty had walked in, so she couldn't quite comprehend what she was saying.

'Aren't your exams coming up?'

'Yes, okay, you can buy it for me after the exams.'

'What is this thing?'

'A video cassette recorder. It's a machine for watching movies. You can watch movies at home. It's not very expensive. I've seen ads on television.'

Farida couldn't figure out whether to laugh or cry at her daughter's self-indulgence. Her audacity was astounding.

'Two days till your exams and you're not worried about that at all. Watching movies at home! I'll slap you so hard, you won't have any teeth left in that mouth of yours. The cheek! Waking me up to ask for a machine to watch movies!'

'You could buy it from Singer. If you buy a VCR from Singer, you get a free iron.'

'Get out of my sight right now! You devil spawn, coming to my room with this nonsense!'

'The free iron's available only for another week.'

'I'm not buying this junk for you.'

'Why not? We do every single thing you say, whether it's fair or unfair. What are we supposed to do, stuck inside this house all day? Indoors, inside this house, let us do whatever we want.' Beauty had spoken in an ice-cold voice and left.

Four days later, Mukhles shaheb had returned from work lugging a VCR and a free iron, and inevitably the VCR was installed in Beauty's room. The VCR was occasionally hauled to the living room, where they would all watch an old Bangla movie together. Not a single movie by the classic romantic duo Uttam-Suchitra was omitted from their family movie nights. These days, they didn't watch anything together anymore. But the mother and the two daughters often watched movies late into the night.

The three of them were supposed to watch *Jodha Akbar* together. Although Beauty was now thinking that she might just go ahead and watch it alone, just to show them how furious she was. On the other hand, she was dying to try some freshly fried, hot luchis. She decided to eat the luchis and then watch the movie. What was the point of punishing herself because she was angry? Beauty didn't feel such stupid anger. She would much rather wield her fury into a situation where nobody but she got to eat any luchis.

Beauty hit the pause button and headed for the dining table. Farida Khanam was waiting there with hot luchis on a plate. She was happy that Beauty had come back. She made a big show of serving and feeding her.

'Amma, aren't you going to make duck curry? Make it spicy.'

'Not too spicy.'

'Why not too spicy?'

'You know your Abba can't stomach it; why do you always argue over everything?'

'Since when does Abba not eat hot food?'

When Beauty was in the mood, she could go on arguing with the utmost devotion. Farida Khanam glared at her daughter for a few moments. Beauty stared back—as if it was a game to see how long they could stare without blinking.

'You're going too far, Beauty. I'm telling you, your days are numbered,' Farida Khanam hissed.

Beauty laughed at her mother's words. Farida Khanam held her gaze for a few moments, and then said in a normal voice, 'I'll fry up a few dried chillies. If you want spicier, you can just work it into your food.'

'Amma, do you want to watch a movie?'

'No, I have to start cooking now. You can watch if you want. You're usually fine watching the same movie multiple times—you can watch it again with us later.'

Farida Khanam left for the kitchen in slow steps. She was feeling a little soothed after the chitchat with her daughter, but her forehead was still wrinkled.

Rabeya's Ma had chopped the onions and prepped everything for lunch before going off to do the laundry. Farida looked everything over and felt satisfied. She placed a large wok on the burner. She poured out a tiny drip of oil; duck had a lot of fat anyway. They had tested Mukhles shaheb's cholesterol last month, and it had been quite high. He should probably stay away from duck meat right now. But if it was cooked, he was surely going to eat a couple of pieces. It didn't feel right to make something that only three people in this family of four could eat.

Even after she separated the wings, the neck and a few bony pieces for Rabeya's Ma and the boy, there was a lot of meat left. Lovely particularly liked the skin. Farida was partial to the skin too; in fact, to be honest, she was the one who relished it the most. But she had never revealed this preference to anyone. During meals, she pretended that she was only giving in to their requests to eat some of it. She decided today she was going to fry the duck in spices for a long time before cooking it well. They would be consuming more fat and spices than usual, but it was fine, it wasn't like they ate like that every day. Also, she had to get started on the hilsa polao. She must remind Rabeya's Ma to make sure everything was ready before she began. Otherwise, at the last minute, she would find out that the fish hadn't even been thawed.

Farida was keeping her mind busy with these banalities. Or she would have been distraught with thoughts of Abdul Bashir. She was aghast that she hadn't thought of Lovely in all this time, or rather she had, perhaps consciously, not allowed thoughts of Lovely in her head. She was certain that Lovely would be back ten or fifteen minutes before the clock struck two; what was the point in driving up her blood pressure with worry?

'I've done the laundry. Give me the roof key, Khalamma, so I can hang up the washing.'

'Have you cut and cleaned the hilsa fish yet?'

'No, I've just put it in water.'

'Cut up the hilsa and clean it properly. Sort through the polao rice, it's full of gravel. It should go on the stove exactly at one so that the food is piping hot when they sit down to eat.'

'Khalamma, the washing?'

'You do exactly what I tell you to and stop your chatter.' When she was done with her long list of instructions, Farida focused on the duck again. Once she had sautéed it well, she poured a little water in the pot and covered it, lowering the flame. 'When the oil floats to the top, turn the stove off.'

Rabeya's Ma, who had been scaling the hilsa in silence, nodded. Farida issued more orders and strode off to the veranda in the back of the house. Before she even got to the veranda, a line from a Hindi song reached her ears, making her squint.

Jo bhi ho tum, khuda ki kasam, la-jawab ho ... Whatever you are, I swear by God, you're beyond compare ...

Mukhles shaheb was almost supine on a cane chair, with his feet resting on a side table. With his eyes shut, he was basking in the bliss of the song and of his head being massaged. The boy was absorbed in plucking grey hairs with a pair of tweezers, his head bobbing to the beat of the song. His lips were moving in sync, but soundlessly.

The boy liked plucking grey hairs. He pulled them out one by one, and kept count while he was at it. Once he reached twenty, he started again. So far, he had plucked three twenties and twelve. Yesterday, he had done two twenties and eighteen; today was much better.

The boy looked alarmed as Farida entered the veranda. Mukhles shaheb was oblivious; perhaps he had fallen asleep. He often snoozed in the veranda like this, with music playing, or with the newspaper spread over his face. Without speaking, Farida gestured at the boy to follow her. She didn't want to bother her husband.

She felt a sort of fondness for the man. He had been planted into this household like an alien tree. He didn't have much to do with the household. He was neither loving nor neglectful towards the girls. His relationship with everything was similar—without attachment. However, he was blind in his dependence on and faith in her. She stared at him tenderly for a few moments. Then she left, instructing the boy to follow her to the roof with the washtub.

'Get all the wet clothes from the bathroom to the roof. Will you be able to carry it all up at one go?'

'Yes, I will.'

'Bring them in the smaller washtub. Where's the key to the gate for the stairs? When you come back from outside, why do you insist on just swallowing the keys? As soon as you come home, you hand over all the keys to me. Understood?'

'Yes.'

'Where's the key? Hand it over.'

'Khalu Jan called me, so then I just put it on the table in the veranda.'

'Go and get it. And then bring the washing to the roof.'

The boy ran off to retrieve the key and suddenly, without warning, Farida's gut churned with the need to know exactly what time it was. The clock on the living room wall had stopped at twelve forty-five three months ago. She hadn't gotten around to replacing the battery yet. Farida almost ran to her bedroom. She glanced at the wall clock across from her bedroom door. Twenty past eleven. She had plenty of time. She struggled to understand why she was so apprehensive. It wasn't really true that she didn't have a clue, though. That phone call from Abdul Bashir had pretty much shaken up her world. Farida had had her fair share of surprises in her life. And she had dealt with everything on her own. But she hadn't been prepared for this morning's shock. Of course, she hadn't been prepared for any of the shocks that life had giver her. But if she had been able to wrest control of those other situations, *insha'allah*, she would be able to take control of this one as well.

She climbed to the roof with quick steps. Who knew why she was rushing! She reached the door to the roof and saw the boy already waiting there, the washing in a large tub at his feet. She unlocked the door. Darkness had congealed in the landing, but a sliver of fierce sunlight was busting its gut under the door, desperate to find a way in. The blinding light leapt in as soon as she opened the door. Farida didn't notice her forehead wrinkling or her eyes squinting. The boy raised a hand to ward off the intensity of the sunlight. Farida felt wonderful as she stepped onto the roof. There was nothing quite like winter sunshine.

'Did you bring the key to the downstairs gate? Hand it over.' She couldn't stop fretting over the keys. She took it from the boy and tied it to her sari-end. Now she felt more at peace.

The boy was hanging up the washing on the clothesline. Farida glanced his way to make sure he was spreading the clothes out tautly. She watched for a while, but soon grew tired. 'Let him do it however he wants to,' she thought, which was very unlike her. Slowly, she walked to the edge of the roof and stood there.

Today was November 16, 2007. Lovely's birthday. She was failing to keep the day under control, no matter how hard she tried. It kept slipping out of her tight grip. Should she tell Mukhles shaheb about Abdul Bashir's call? But what good would that do? Telling him or not didn't make much difference. Anyway, his health hadn't been so good in recent weeks.

'Khalamma, I want to go downstairs.'

'Yes, go. Tell Rabeya's Ma that I'll begin the hilsa polao as soon as I'm down. You go and clean up the table and wash up the plates and glasses.'

The boy left. The sound of his feet stomping down the stairs faded. Farida was completely alone on the rooftop now. She paced from one end to the other, twice.

--

Farida had returned to her father's house carrying Lovely; she was eight months and nine days pregnant. This was her second visit to her father's house since her wedding. In between, almost two years had gone by. She had neither visited nor written to her parents. The handful of times that Mukhles shaheb had proposed a visit, Farida had given him a straight answer: 'After marriage, a woman no longer belongs to her father's house; her husband's home becomes everything to her. Why are you itching to go to my father's house anyway? If it bothers you that much, why don't *you* go and visit them?'

After a customary scolding like that, Mukhles shaheb wouldn't prolong the conversation. But then, one day, Farida herself wanted to go. She was heavily pregnant by then. Mukhles shaheb was taking care of Farida as best as he could. However, instead of making her happy, he was mostly getting berated for his attempts to figure out what to do and what not to do for her. It was the best time in her life. It had also been good when she was pregnant with Beauty, but it didn't compare with that first experience. Not for a moment did it seem to either Farida or Mukhles shaheb that there was anything amiss between them.

Mukhles shaheb had already written to Farida's mother, giving her the good news. Farida's mother had opened the letter with some trepidation—it had been a while since they had received any news of their daughter. She held her breath as she read the letter from beginning to end. The corner of her mouth twitched as she read it, but only momentarily. The next moment, her face lit up with a smile, like the gradual dawning of light at daybreak. The aura of that light had persisted until the last day of Farida's visit to her parents. She felt an immense pride in her daughter. If that wasn't her girl!

It was mid-October when Farida had arrived at her father's house to deliver her child. The enormous house at Kapasia was in a frenzy. As if no one else had ever had a baby before.

Fall! The aroma of freshly harvested rice permeated the yard. The day-labourer women hummed while they worked at the rice thresher. Every morning there were rice cakes made from the new rice, fresh date-palm sap, and the pulp from green coconuts. Divine comfort and joy. Three young women were at Farida's beck and call at all times. One kneaded her head with hair oil, another made dried fish and jackfruit-seed paste for her, while the third kept the stove alive for warm compresses for her belly. Both of Farida's sisters-in-law lived at the Kapasia house back then. Her younger sister hadn't yet been married off. The care and comfort provided to Farida made all three envious, especially Farida's younger sister Shirin.

Farida's mother had always been a measured person. Her presence granted even an ordinary scene a special gravity. Thus, it was her sudden immoderation that everyone remarked upon. Farida's wasn't the first baby in their family—both her brothers and her elder sister had already had babies. At least two each. No one quite understood what the big deal was about Farida having a baby. It triggered jealousy all around. Every morning and evening, with great devotion, Farida's mother massaged sesame oil on Farida's belly to prevent stretchmarks. She bathed Farida in warm water. She cooked Farida's favourite dishes. She did everything she could. She combed her hair, weaving it into braids. She stuck to Farida like a shadow. Her mother's care made Farida realise that, by all measures, she was equal to her blessed mother. She held her head higher than before, much higher than was good for her.

--

Caw, caw, caw.

The coarse cawing of the crows jerked her back to the present. Farida looked up and saw a crow circling low around their roof. She couldn't see any other crows nearby. She swung an arm at it shouting 'whoosh ... whoosh' to scare it off. It didn't work. Instead, the crow grew more desperate. It began to circle right above her at a dangerous proximity, continuing its raucous cawing. It was a solitary afternoon; not a soul could be seen on any of the neighbouring rooftops. And here was this crow, cawing endlessly. In the afternoon as undisturbed as a still lake, the crow's hoarse call seemed to emerge from another world, existing only to send her a warning.

She was consumed with the desire to get rid of the creature. She picked up a piece of rubble from a corner of the roof and lobbed it at the crow. It didn't even get close; it fell back halfway up. The crow didn't even notice it. Farida wondered if another crow had died somewhere nearby. But, no, if that had been the case, there would be other crows with this one. Her sense of dread returned with renewed strength.

Spied from far above, the rooftop scene would look like this: a lonely rooftop, crushed by the surrounding silence, and on that rooftop, an even lonelier middle-aged woman, running blindly, as if without direction, shouting 'whoosh ... whoosh', with her arms raised above her head. Above her circled a crow like black velvet, cawing without pause. Something was about to happen, something really bad was about to happen—the foreboding crashed into Farida's mind again and again, like a river breaking its banks, and each time, the gamut of her rage settled on the crow. As if she could free herself from all the misfortune about to descend on her and her family if only she could get rid of this crow.

--

Beauty couldn't focus on the movie. Various possibilities about what she could worm out of Farida Khanam kept circling in her head. It had to be something expensive. A certain fear needed to be fed into Amma's heart, every day, bit by bit, so that finally she was primed to render unto Beauty whatever she desired. Then, when the moment was right, it was merely a question of showing up with her demand. For Beauty, by now, finagling things out of Farida Khanam was as easy as taking candy from a baby. Of course, so far, she hadn't squeezed her mother for anything too big. The priciest thing she had ever got was the VCR. But this time, she would have to go after something that only she herself could use and enjoy. What could she ask for? She could demand a television with a huge screen ... but, no, not a television set. Everyone would be crowding her room all the time. Who knows, maybe even their father would show up with his cane chair and settle himself in there.

What on earth made Amma let her sister go out by herself, what on earth! Why did Apa need to go to Gausia by herself? Beauty couldn't bring herself to swallow Amma's decision to send Lovely outside on her own. If she now asked to open the door and go downstairs, if she wanted to go out and take a walk around their neighbourhood, Amma wouldn't allow it—not in a million years. She had never disobeyed their mother. Lovely had been brazen enough to be friendly, to even have a relationship with someone—all Beauty had ever accomplished was pointless arguments with Amma. She knew there was no harm in her bickering; Farida Khanam knew it as well.

When Beauty had given Farida Khanam the lowdown on Riaz, she'd thought that Lovely's time was up. Just as it should have been. But Farida Khanam barely did anything to her. The two of them were locked in their rooms for eighteen days—that was it. If Beauty had pulled a stunt like that, assault or even murder wouldn't have been surprising. But this time, there would be a reckoning. She wasn't going to let this go.

Beauty couldn't understand why everyone treated her like that. For instance, she was three and a half years younger than Lovely. Not one, not two, but three and a half! And yet Riaz had barely glanced at her. He had turned love-crazed for Lovely, like the Prophet Yusuf for Julekha in the epics. She could swear that she was ten times prettier than Lovely, and she took care of herself too. So what was the mystery? Lovely kept up a façade that she didn't understand anything, didn't know anything—and Amma was taken in by that. But Beauty knew how sly Lovely really was. Who knew what she was up to today. If Amma kept Beauty locked up, then she should shackle Apa's entire body, top to toe.

Beauty burned as these thoughts crossed her mind. She jerked herself up from bed and turned off the television. 'Rabeya's Ma! Rabeya's Ma!'

'What?'

'Where's Amma?'

'She went up to the roof with ...'

Beauty zoomed out of her room like a night train before Rabeya's Ma had finished speaking. She crashed into the boy as she rushed to the roof. The boy was clambering down the stairs while Beauty hurtled up. Head-on collision. The boy was hurt more. He slid down onto the stairs from the impact. Beauty barely glanced at him. She threw a swearword at him before resuming her charge upwards.

A strange scene greeted her as she stepped onto the roof, rooting her to the spot. She watched dumbstruck as her mother ran in circles like a mad woman, throwing up her arms again and again as a crow followed her.

Once, it looked like the crow was about to peck her. The crow kept swooping downwards, close to Farida Khanam's head, but then she whooshed at it and it flew upwards again. What she saw of her mother shocked her. The abnormality of their entire lives lit up like neon signs. Beauty felt despair—for Farida, and for Lovely and herself. Quietly, without alerting her mother to her presence, she went back downstairs.

Although Beauty had barged up the stairs so loudly, Farida didn't notice her at all. She was engrossed in getting rid of the crow. Finally, the crow grew tired and settled itself on the next roof; but it wouldn't stop cawing. With the crow surrendering the fight, Farida stood there like a fool. She realised that the insides of her blouse were soaking wet. Panting, she gripped the railing. When the wheezing in her chest slowed down to a bearable level, she left the rooftop, although what she wanted to do was run away. Still, she shut the door, turned the key, and climbed down the stairs. Who knew for whom she put on this display of being calm and controlled. Perhaps for herself. It was important to let herself know that she was still mentally strong, that she wouldn't bow her head so easily.

Back in the house, Farida's bluster redoubled. She could hear the television blaring from Beauty's room; she went there first.

A different movie was playing. Beauty was half lying, half sitting in bed, pretending to watch *Munna Bhai MBBS*. She had watched it at least ten times. Beauty couldn't decide whether to smile at Farida or ignore her and keep staring at the television. In the end, she looked at her mother.

'Hey, get up. Turn that off.'

'Why?'

'No chores, no nothing—all you ever do is watch movies. You're just a piece of rubbish.'

'What am I supposed to do?'

'If you've got nothing to do, then get up and just walk around. Doesn't your back hurt from lying down all the time?'

'No, it doesn't.' Beauty had no intention of getting into an argument. But even though there were other people in the house, Farida Khanam attacked her, which made her veins flood with rage. 'Get out of my way. You're blocking my view.'

This time, when Farida Khanam glared at her, Beauty ignored her. She laughed aloud at some dialogue in the movie. Farida Khanam became composed as usual.

'Haven't you seen this movie several times already? And you still laugh at it? You're an idiot.'

'It's a funny movie. What am I supposed to do—sit here with a sour face?'

Farida Khanam had begun tidying the messy clothes hanging from the clothes rack. Beauty glanced at her from the corner of her eye. She couldn't get the rooftop scene out of her mind. Yet there was no sign now that mere minutes ago, Farida had come unglued.

'Is your Abba going to visit his village home?'

'Does he even have a village home? What home is he supposed to visit?'

'What do you mean what home ... if nothing else, at least there's his ancestral homestead. The other heirs have sent news after all this time—apparently your father also has a share there. Most of the family is already dead anyway. What I say is, there's no need to go. He'll be travelling alone. If something happens on the way, that'll be it.'

'Why did you let Apa go by herself?'

'I don't know that myself.' For the first time since morning, Farida spoke the truth. She truly did not know what had led to this lapse. Was this a symptom of some kind?

'What if Apa doesn't come back?'

'Why do such bad thoughts pop up in your head? If she doesn't come back—where would she go? Does she have anywhere to go? If she did, you would know. So, tell me, does she?'

'She might.'

Farida gripped Beauty's chin. Beauty was amused. There was absolutely no trace in her of the heartache she had felt for her mother just moments ago.

Looking at Beauty's eyes and her smile, Farida realised that her daughter was playing with her. She hissed, 'You're a devil among devils. Your days are numbered ...'

'Everyone's days are numbered. Most of all, yours.'

Farida let go of her chin. Beauty returned to her movie. The next scene was very funny. Farida made to leave.

'Amma, tell Rabeya's Ma to make some more lentil paste and put it in the fridge. There's no more left.'

'Okay, I will.' Farida turned back. 'What time is it? Aren't you going to say your prayers?'

At the mention of prayers, Beauty jumped out of bed. She hadn't performed her ablutions yet. Farida went towards her own bedroom. She might as well cook the hilsa polao after her prayers.

She stretched herself out on her bed for a few minutes with her eyes closed. As she lay there, she thought about turning the cellphone back on. Who was she so scared of that she had turned the phone off? Farida wasn't scared of worthless people. She took her time climbing out of bed and walking to her dressing table. She gazed at her reflection in the mirror and suddenly realised how stunning she had once been.

Time and circumstance made even the most desirable person inconsequential—she suffered no cheap guilt over that. She had done everything necessary to create the veneer of a conventional life. She didn't feel like a sinner. Why would she ...? She was, however, troubled by today's intrusion after all this time.

She turned the cellphone back on. Trying to avoid a problem only allowed it to ensconce itself further, so it was better to face it head-on. She would see how far either of them were willing to go.

Mukhles shaheb entered the room. He wanted to perform his prayers too. He glanced twice at his wife's face. Farida looked distressed, but he was too scared to ask what was going on. Today many things were happening for the first time ever anyway. He still couldn't quite believe that Farida had allowed Lovely to go out by herself.

'Bashir called.'

'Who's Bashir?'

'Are you joking? You don't know who Bashir is?'

What was going on? What did Bashir want after all this time? Mukhles shaheb assumed a hangdog expression. He didn't like trouble. All he wanted to do was sit in the veranda, jiggling his legs, while enjoying some Hindi music, watch a movie or two now and then, do the grocery shopping sometimes, and eat well—that is all he asked of life. What aggravation was this! 'What does he want?'

'He's bubbling over with love all of a sudden. He wants to see Lovely and Beauty ... I'll show him. If I don't gouge his eyes out with date-palm thorns, my name isn't Farida.'

Mukhles shaheb preferred not to remain in the presence of a wrathful Farida. He slipped into the bathroom to perform his pre-prayer ablutions. It was better to not get involved. Farida would surely take care of everything by herself. His involvement would merely complicate things further. And, surprisingly, he no longer felt any anxiety. That was dangerous, though. He should hang on to his concerned face a few more days, at least in front of Farida.

Farida was annoyed with herself. Why share all this with this half-dead man, she thought. What she wanted was for Abdul Bashir to call again right then. They could hash it all out. What the hell would he achieve by seeing Lovely and Beauty? Would he be able to keep them with him? Would he be able to tell the truth to his sons or the rest of his family? So what did Farida have to be afraid of?

'Khalamma, aren't you going to do the cooking?' Rabeya's Ma called to her.

'I'm coming. I'm coming as soon as I've said my prayers. You go on. Has the boy watered the plants in the balcony? If he hasn't, tell him to do it now.'

Farida waited for Mukhles shaheb. She decided that when he emerged from the bathroom, she would not utter another word on the topic of Bashir.

--

Lovely was born at eight thirty-two in the morning. Mukhles shaheb had recorded the time and date in a green notebook. A couple of days after the birth, Farida's elder sister-in-law had said in a joking manner, 'Our Farida and her husband are both quite fair. So how did this baby girl get such a dark complexion?'

Her words had barely left her mouth when Farida's mother pounced on her like a lioness. 'No, she won't stay so dark. Her complexion will lighten up with time. Of course, my father-in-law himself had skin like ebony.'

Shamed by her mother-in-law's words, the sister-in-law had bit her tongue. She was also taken aback. Because her mother-in-law usually did not participate in such trivial banter. And she knew that her grandfather-in-law's complexion had definitely not been like ebony. She had seen him. Although by then he was on his way to his grave, she clearly remembered that he hadn't even been slightly dark, let alone like ebony.

From that day onwards, Farida's mother had made a point of commenting on how strongly the newborn Lovely resembled Mukhles shaheb. She even discovered similarities in their expressions and smiles.

--

Mukhles shaheb emerged quietly from the bathroom. He avoided eye contact with Farida and went straight to the prayer mat. Two prayer mats were always laid out in their room. The tops of the mats, where they touched their foreheads in *shezda*, were kept folded down; they just rolled it back up before performing their *namaaz*. Mukhles shaheb crouched and straightened the *shezda* spot on his mat, and then stood up straight to begin his *namaaz*.

Farida was watching Mukhles shaheb intently. Now she too entered the bathroom to perform her *oju*, the pre-prayer ablutions. She was making mistakes again and again. It took her three tries to finish the *oju* the way she was supposed to. Done, she left the bathroom.

She finished her prayers and sat for a long time with her hands raised in *monajat*. But she didn't beg Allah for anything specific. Suddenly she felt very small; it felt humiliating to ask even Allah for something. A feeling of intransigence reared its head. No, she would not entreat anyone for anything, not even Allah. The life she had already endured—how much more complicated could it become? If it did, she would see it through.

Farida stood up and stepped off her prayer mat. She stooped and folded back the top. Then she unconsciously made the *tauba* gesture of contrition, and went and stood in front of the wardrobe, gazing at the cellphone. Several moments passed and then, with a twisted smile on her lips, she left her bedroom. As if someone had competed with her and lost.

——

Beauty turned the movie back on after she was done with her prayers, but she wasn't enjoying it anymore. How many times could she laugh at the same scene? She turned the TV and the DVD player off. She glared at the clock: five minutes past one. Not long before Apa returned. Only Allah knew what crap she had bought. Beauty was quite certain that she would like none of it. Beauty and Lovely's tastes never matched. Lovely always preferred muted colours, while Beauty loved vivid hues: red, magenta, fuchsia. Beauty wore her hair loose, while Lovely's perennial style was two long braids.

She had no sense of fashion. Beauty took care of herself. She plucked her eyebrows, painted her nails. Lovely liked Riaz, while for the life of her, Beauty couldn't see what was attractive about Riaz. However, even though she didn't like Riaz, she also didn't like it that Riaz had chosen Lovely over her.

If she thought about it seriously, she found that she didn't really like anyone. The person she disliked the most was Mukhles shaheb. She didn't know why. Beauty had no idea where this intense hatred for her own father had come from. Of course, nobody in the household knew. Because just as she didn't like anyone, she also didn't trust anyone. Her own room was her most favourite place. She liked it there. She didn't even like spending time in another room, never mind going outdoors. Although she was ready for Chinese food day or night. Once a month, Farida Khanam, Lovely and she went out to eat. On those days, she felt like a happy person.

Beauty thought of playing the game with Apa tonight. What if they changed it up a little? Tonight, they could play in Apa's room. Tonight, they could target their father instead of their mother. She would see whether it was Apa or she who got him in the end. First, Apa could play their father, then it would be her turn to play him.

As she thought about the game, Beauty grew excited. The unbearable smell of hilsa polao drifted over from the kitchen. The thought that she would have to eat it in a little while made her retch. Only Allah knew whose birthday she was going to ruin some day, Lovely's or her own, by yanking off the plastic tablecloth. She wasn't even going to touch that fucking polao today; she was only going to eat the duck curry. There would most certainly also be brown rice. The thought of food made her hungry. But they couldn't eat before Apa got back; although that wouldn't be too long.

The aroma of food gradually drew Beauty out of her room. The boy was humming some song as he set the table. Who knew whether he had bought the stuff or not. He was in deep trouble if he hadn't brought it today. That imp had been stalling for three days straight, telling her today, tomorrow, the day after. The stuff wasn't anything outrageous, it was just marijuana. Beauty wasn't a pothead; she merely puffed on a joint now and then in the bathroom. She enjoyed it. She had been smoking for about a year now. The boy had introduced her to it. As her mind wandered, it occurred to Beauty that their father must have given Apa some money today. She would have to wangle at least five hundred from that.

Every month, Farida Khanam gave Lovely and Beauty a thousand takas each. Lovely barely used any of it. Sometimes she ordered in fuchka or ice cream; she also liked pastries from Cooper's. But those cost nothing. The rest of the money she spent on Beauty. But then most of the food she got also ended up in Beauty's belly. Even Mukhles shaheb grew gleeful when Cooper's pastries showed up at their house. Anything sweet was poison for him because of his diabetes. But they *had* to give him a pastry, and that too keeping it secret from Farida Khanam.

Beauty always exhausted her pocket-money before the month was over. She bought two or three DVDs every week. It was usually Lovely who went out with Farida Khanam to pick up the latest Hindi films. Beauty also subscribed to three cine magazines—two Indian, one Bangladeshi. Although she was the subscriber, even Mukhles shaheb got to read them. Ugh!

Every inch of her skin burned with annoyance if Mukhles shaheb used anything that belonged to her. But thanks to her stellar acting, nobody at home had an inkling. For instance, when pastries were brought in, Beauty always insisted on giving at least half of her share to Mukhles shaheb. She never allowed Lovely to share hers.

'It's okay, Apa. Both of you adore these pastries. I don't like them all that much. Let me share mine.'

Although Lovely's heart softened at this uncharacteristic tenderness, Beauty would be thinking to herself: Eat, you old geezer, guzzle till you die. If I could, I'd ram an entire cake down your throat.

--

The boy was decanting pickles from the jar into a bowl. He was being very careful not to look at Beauty.

'Hey, *shoytan*, did you get the candles? I've been telling you to get candles for three days now—hasn't it reached your ears yet?'

'Candle' was their codename for marijuana. After thinking it over, Beauty had decided that this was the most unsuspicious name. With the frequent power outages, candles were the only thing she could send the boy out for repeatedly.

Farida Khanam finished her cooking and entered the dining room. 'Why do you need a candle now? I've got a few in my room, go and take one from there.'

'No, why should I take yours? I told him to bring some, so I want to see if he's brought them. If he hasn't, he's in for it. Hey, you brat, did you get them?'

'Yes, I did. I left them in your room.'

'When?'

'When you went up to the roof.'

'When did you go to the roof?' Farida Khanam asked.

'When you were running after that crow.'

Beauty's response halted Farida Khanam momentarily, but she rallied quickly. 'Didn't I tell you not to go to the roof without asking me first?'

'You were on the roof. How was I supposed to ask you? Rabeya's Ma said you were there, so I went up.'

Farida Khanam glared at Beauty and left. Beauty didn't care. She bustled off quickly towards her bedroom to look for the 'candles'. First, she locked her door. Then she pulled out the marijuana sticks stuck behind the mirror of her dressing table as usual. There were only two. She had given that son of a bitch a hundred takas, and he had brought back only two. He was jerking her around. 'I'll show you to mess with me, just wait,' Beauty said aloud. She tucked the blunts back behind the mirror. She decided to smoke up in the evening. The wall clock chimed twice right then. The realisation that it was two o'clock already paralysed her for a few moments. Then she ran and opened the door. Apa wasn't back yet—she leaned against the door like a wooden doll. Farida Khanam was nowhere to be seen. Step by step, Beauty approached her mother's room.

Farida had been losing control of her anxiety for a while now. She had believed in her heart that Lovely would be home at least fifteen minutes before the clock struck two. But there was no sign of her. What should she do now, where could she search? No, she had to maintain an unflustered front. No one should glimpse the turmoil inside her.

When Beauty entered the room, Farida was sitting on the cane chair by the street-side window, as still as a statue. She seemed unaware that Beauty had entered her room. Mukhles shaheb was nowhere to be seen. He had probably holed up somewhere as soon as it turned two, waiting for the apocalypse to strike.

Eventually, Farida became aware of Beauty's presence. The two of them stared at each other for several moments. Beauty broke the silence.

'Amma, I'm hungry. Aren't we going to eat?'

'Yes, tell Rabeya's Ma to serve the food. Tell her to make a tomato salad.'

'Okay.'

'Go and see where your father is, and tell him to come to the table. He shouldn't be eating so late.' Her attempt to remain normal made her words sound brusque and cold. Neither mentioned Lovely. As if girls from this family going out by themselves and not returning on time was something that happened every day. Beauty went out to deliver the instructions to Rabeya's Ma. As she was about to exit, she bumped into the door jamb and almost lost her footing. She clutched the door and balanced herself, looking back at Farida with a smile that said 'silly me!', and awkwardly scratched her head. Farida said nothing. Instead, Beauty's smile made her furrow her brows even further.

She was seeing ill omens everywhere. That cursed girl, couldn't she have found a better time to stumble? She was the devil, that's what she was. Farida repeated the words to herself several times. She looked at the wall clock again in disbelief. Seven minutes past two—how was this even possible?

Beauty went to the kitchen and found that Rabeya's Ma was already making tomato salad. Farida Khanam didn't approve of people doing things before she told them to. She loathed pushy people. So how come Rabeya's Ma was making tomato salad before the order had arrived?

'What are you doing, Rabeya's Ma?'

'I'm chopping the tomatoes, Chhoto Apa, for the salad.'

'Did Amma tell you to make the salad?'

'No, she didn't. But every year I make tomato salad on your birthdays. No cucumbers, only tomatoes.'

'Don't try to be a smartass. Don't do anything until you're told. Do you understand?'

'Don't you want a tomato salad?'

'Why wouldn't I want tomato salad? I'm just warning you, don't be a smartass. Will you remember that?'

'Yes, I will.'

'Serve the food. Where's that boy?'

'Cleaning the bathroom.'

She would have to go after that boy. She would have to get to the bottom of how two joints could cost a hundred. What was this, a free for all? People could just do whatever they wanted?

Beauty stomped off to her room. The clock on the wall she was facing stared back at her in mockery. Look, Beauty, look! Your prissy, goody two shoes elder sister has done what you failed to do with all your big talk. Your hot air balloon just got pricked.

Beauty felt an unbearable fury against herself—unbearable. She had spent all these years sitting pretty at home. Of course, she had; they couldn't haul her out of the house with a crane. What was she so scared of? Why did she turn into a worm outside of these stifling walls? Her skin crawled in repulsion and self-hatred. No matter what bluster she doled out at home, the moment she stepped outside she curled up like a worm. As she comprehended this truth for the first time, she felt small. Her desire to tear into the boy completely disappeared.

When the boy came out of the bathroom, he cocked an eyebrow at her, wanting to know how the sticks were. Beauty was stunned at his audacity. It seemed that she was the only one in this house who had no guts.

'Why are there only two joints?'

'Hakim Bhai's out of stock at the moment. He gave me these from his own stash. You're owed two more.'

'Why did you give him all the money then?'

'I didn't. I still have enough for a couple more joints with me. I didn't give it back to you because I have to go back tomorrow or the day after to pick up the other two.'

'Go and call Abba. Tell him the food has been served.'

'Where's Boro Khala? She's still not back.'

'Don't stand here and blather, you brat. Go on, get out of this room right now.'

'I was just asking because I was worried.'

As soon as the boy left, Beauty felt an intense desire to go into the bathroom to toke up. But she couldn't do it now. She was about to be summoned for lunch any moment. This damned life—she couldn't do anything she wanted to.

Their dining room was very neatly organised for a small space. It wasn't really a proper room, but sort of a common space linking the different rooms in the house. The dining space was adjacent to the kitchen, and across from the kitchen were two doors side by side—one led to Lovely's room, the other to Beauty's.

Beyond their rooms, at the end of the passage were two more rooms, like the top half of the letter Y. The one on the left was the sitting room, and the one on the right was Farida Khanam and Mukhles shaheb's bedroom. This was the largest room in the house. Both the sitting room and the master bedroom faced the street. Farida Khanam's bedroom gave a clearer view of the street than the sitting room.

The dining space contained a dining table with six chairs. The head of the table was fixed for Mukhles shaheb. Farida Khanam sat to his left, with Lovely beside her, and Beauty across from her. The meat-safe and the refrigerator were also in that room. On the wall to the left hung a framed picture of the holy site of Ajmer Sharif.

The food was already on the table. Everything was steaming hot. The aroma was thickening the air in the room. Beauty couldn't keep her hunger in check anymore. She was desperate. She sat down in her chair and shouted for Farida Khanam. Although she had no desire to call Mukhles shaheb, she had to. They couldn't begin to eat until he joined. Perfect, everything had to be perfect.

'Why are you shouting?'

'I'm hungry. It was two o'clock ages ago.'

Why did she say that? Why remind her mother of something like that? Both mother and daughter glanced at the wall clock. However, the clock was stuck at twelve forty-five. Allah's grace! It was better not to witness that time had continued to rush forward despite already hitting the two o'clock mark.

'Rabeya's Ma, haven't I told you to stay close by at mealtimes? Remove Lovely's plate.'

Rabeya's Ma hesitated before taking it away. Farida Khanam looked at Beauty and explained her decision: 'I don't like looking at an empty plate ... Bring it back when Lovely returns.' The last bit was directed at Rabeya's Ma. She placed the plate on top of the meat-safe instead of inside the cabinet.

'Call your Khalu Jan.'

'The boy's gone to get him,' Beauty informed her.

Farida Khanam pulled the serving dish of duck curry towards herself and sniffed it. She seemed quite satisfied. 'Rabeya's Ma, bring the pot of meat over here. And your bowls.'

Rabeya's Ma immediately came out of the kitchen, carrying the cooking pot and the bowls, as if she had been waiting behind the door, ready with those things. Farida Khanam was pleased at this promptness. In addition to the neck pieces and the wings, she even gave each of them a meaty piece of duck, a piece of skin and some sauce. Had she suddenly become generous today, or were her thoughts in such disarray that she was doling out meat for even the servants? Even Rabeya's Ma's eyes grew round when she looked at the bowls. 'Khalamma, is this curry for me and the boy?'

'Less talk, okay? This curry is for now and tonight. Take these bowls away and bring another plate.'

'Okay.'

'You haven't cooked rice for yourselves, have you?'

'No.' Rabeya's Ma's teeth were bared in a grin as she said no. Mukhles shaheb entered the room quietly like a cat, and slid into his chair. He directed a goofy smile at Beauty—and immediately her face hardened.

Even if nobody else knew that Beauty couldn't stand Mukhles shaheb, the fact was clear as day to the man himself. But he too had never allowed it to become public knowledge. He bore it as if it was a very common situation—as if there was nothing surprising about a daughter harbouring hatred for her father; it happened all the time.

In the second round, Farida Khanam shocked Rabeya's Ma and the rest of them again by doling out two good pieces of hilsa fish and a heap of polao rice for the servants. Oh, Farida's heart was certainly tender today—Mukhles shaheb tried to swallow back the deep sigh that was escaping with this thought and choked. He gulped down a mouthful of water to control his gagging.

Beauty thought to herself: After all this time, Amma just got caught out. The corner of her lips twisted into a smile, which disappeared immediately, like the sun peeking through clouds.

They ate in silence. Other than the *chapat-chapat* sound of Mukhles shaheb munching, there was no other noise. Today's hilsa polao was exceptionally delicious. Beauty could tell from the smell when she reached the table that it was going to be amazing. As soon as Farida Khanam was done with doling out the meal for Rabeya's Ma and the boy, Beauty had pretty much attacked the food. Mukhles shaheb was also devouring everything with deep enjoyment. Only Farida Khanam bit her lips twice as she ate, shivered twice for no reason, and tipped her glass before it was close enough to her mouth, spilling water on her sari. Although she was slightly discomfited, she covered up the awkwardness with considerable skill, or so she thought. Only once did Beauty pause while ferrying food to her mouth with her fingers and look at her mother. She looked away as quickly as she could in case her mother's misery made her laugh again.

'Rabeya's Ma, bring the bowls of rice pudding and sweet curd from the fridge.'

Nobody ate rice pudding or sweet curd that afternoon. Mukhles shaheb had wanted to, but he wasn't allowed any. Beauty had wolfed everything down until she was stuffed to her gills. She didn't have an inch in her belly that wasn't full. She left the table saying she would have some later in the afternoon. Farida Khanam herself felt nauseated as soon as she looked at the dessert bowl; there was no way she could eat any.

Everyone, except Mukhles shaheb, went to their own rooms as soon as lunch was over. He had decided to somehow or other stay out of Farida Khanam's line of sight. He would emerge from his veranda once Lovely was back home and the ensuing apocalypse was over. He could also sit in the living room, but it was very dark in there. The veranda was a better location; even in winter, there was plenty of light and air. He decided to take a thick wrap with him and settle himself in the veranda. He knew that neither Farida Khanam nor Beauty would be able to tolerate his presence right now. Their tempers would flare the moment they saw him. What was the point in upsetting them for no reason? He could sit quietly in the veranda and listen to his music at a low volume. Or, no, today it was probably a bad idea to listen to music. It didn't matter; new issues of the cine magazines had arrived. He could easily spend an hour or two thumbing through them. He might even take a nap. The boy would show up as soon as he went to the veranda, greedy for tips. He could ask him to either massage his head or pluck a few more grey hairs. The boy would gently tug at his hair, and it would lull him to sleep.

--

Clouds had been massing for a long time above House No. 115/3, Monipuripara. It was hard to say where they were gathering from above this one particular house on this winter's afternoon. But it was clear that they were riding here on the black velvet bodies of the crows. Like armed soldiers dismounting from trucks, they dropped off one by one when they reached the house.

As if, with the clouds above and the residents trapped inside, this house stood paused in front of an undeniable punctuation mark.

Clouds were massing inside Farida's head as well. Dense, clotted clouds. Sometimes they tried to force their way out through her forehead, just between her two eyebrows, like a rhinoceros horn; sometimes the clouds rumbled. The pulsing of her forehead, bulging and contracting, was visible. She couldn't even tell whether her head was aching. Amid all this, she still felt grateful towards Mukhles shaheb; after all, he was letting her be right now. If Mukhles shaheb hung around her at this moment, invariably she would take out all her hatred, anger and frustration on him.

Farida had been pacing from one end of her bedroom to the other for the past fifteen minutes. She didn't want to look at the clock. She wouldn't be surprised if it was four by now. She couldn't even sit down quietly to think; her brain wasn't working. At times she couldn't even remember what she was supposed to think about. It was beyond her imagination that Lovely could ever behave with such desperation. What if, just as Beauty had said, she never came back? But where could she go? For forty years, she had cared for this girl, nurtured her. Could this girl betray her so atrociously? What hadn't she done for her daughters? She had maintained barely any relationship with the rest of her family, she didn't bother with any social niceties. She was sacrificing her life to make sure that her daughters enjoyed all creature comforts. Nothing took priority over their needs and their safety. What else could she have done for them? She hadn't even married them off. Her anxiety over what kind of life lay in store for them after marriage hadn't allowed any of the prospective grooms to remain in play for too long.

The phone had been ringing for a while. It rang five times before it stopped, but Farida didn't hear it at all. It began ringing again. This time she ran to the phone, but she didn't pick up. She stood frozen beside the wardrobe. She reached out once, but withdrew her hand.

It began ringing again. Whoever was calling wasn't about to give up.

'Hello?'

'Hello.'

'Yes, talk. Tell me what is it you want?'

'I've never asked for anything, Farida.'

'This is not the moment to kid around. You're calling me after twenty, or was it twenty-two, years—you must have some agenda. The sooner you admit what it is, the better it is for both of us.'

'You haven't changed even a bit, Farida. As hard as steel.'

'Please stop this pointless whining.'

'I just want to see the girls, Farida. I won't tell them who I am or anything else. I just want to see them with my own eyes, that's all.'

'Impossible.'

'I've done my duty, Farida, now you do yours. We've both grown old. My health is failing. I'll be summoned to Allah's presence any day now. If I could just see the girls, it would bring me some peace.'

'I told you already, that will never be possible. And who are you trying this nonsense on—what duty? What you're doing is an act of contrition for your sins, nothing more. Will you be able to stand before your children and tell them who Lovely and Beauty are? Can you?'

'No, I can't bring them that kind of grief at this age. It hasn't been that long since Khodeja passed away. I won't harm anyone. I just want to come and see them. I wanted to leave them some money.'

'If you want to leave them money, do it. I will come and collect it on their behalf. But you're not going to meet the girls.' Farida's voice rang hard and cold as steel.

Abdul Bashir was silent for a few moments after Farida spoke. Then he sighed. 'Even having the two girls couldn't make you happy, Farida?'

'Who's given you this newsflash that I am unhappy?'

Once more Abdul Bashir remained silent for several seconds. Only his laboured breathing sounded from the other end. The clouds massed tightly below Farida's brows seemed to be loosening. Any moment now, intense lightning would call forth torrential rain, or the dense clouds would be blown away by the wind, giving Farida the chance to become harder and tougher.

'Why didn't you let the girls get married, Farida? Why did you harm them this way? I can't sleep at night thinking about them ...'

He was probably still talking, but Farida no longer had the energy to listen. She disconnected. She placed her hands on the wardrobe and rested her head on them. After a while, she slid onto the floor beside the wardrobe. Tears dripped from her eyes. Farida didn't stop them. Let all of it come out.

How she had shielded the girls every livelong day that Allah had created! She had sheltered them the way hens kept their chicks under their wings. Farida found most things in the world disgusting, they turned her stomach—she had let none of that touch either of her girls. Nobody understood that she was saving her girls. And it was fine that nobody understood. She couldn't be bothered with other people. The real consideration was that her girls were okay.

Farida recalled that Lovely wasn't home yet. Her heart wanted to leap out of her chest. In a flash, she grew certain about Lovely's exact whereabouts. No matter how much he tried to mislead her with these phone calls, she could swear that Lovely was now in the hands of Abdul Bashir.

Was he going to tell her everything? No, he wouldn't do that. So what was he going to tell her?

Farida wanted to run from her room. She wanted to go to Beauty's room and sit there, quietly clasping her daughter's hand. If someone locked them in there right then, even better.

Where were Lovely and Bashir at this moment? What was Lovely doing? Had she eaten anything for lunch? She must have. Bashir would surely have fed her. He had probably taken her to some fancy restaurant. He had to show off his wealth to her, didn't he? What if Lovely didn't want to come back after hearing the whole story? What if she didn't want to see her mother's face again? No, that could never happen. Return she would. After all, she was Farida's daughter. Neither sister had ever learned to disobey Farida.

--

After her *naiyor*, the post-wedding visit to her father's house, Farida had settled down with her husband in his house at the far end of Kobi Jashimuddin Road in Kamlapur.

Knowing the disappointment and humiliation with which his new bride had left for her father's house, Mukhles shaheb had assumed that there was zero possibility of her return. But when she did come back to him, that too seemingly with a smile, he was baffled. To live with an absolutely gorgeous, full-fledged woman was a horrifying proposition.

'I really didn't want to get married, Farida. You can ask your elder brother.'

'Listen, you're my husband. Your shame is my shame. We are never going to talk about this again. This conversation ends today, just remember that.'

'How are you going to get through life?'

'Listen, let me tell you a true story. It's about my own cousin. The day after her wedding, her husband was bitten by a snake. She spent the rest of her life at her in-laws', at the beck and call of all and sundry. In comparison, I am a blessed woman. My husband is alive and well. So not another word about this.'

Farida set up her home in the three-room house with a tin roof. She really liked the place. It was right in the heart of the city, but there was a rural air about it. A small shed adjacent to the main house was the kitchen. In the sliver of space next to it stood a tube-well set in a cement plinth. That was where the washing up, of pots and pans and hands and mouths, took place. They grew vegetables in the large patch of empty ground behind the house. On weekends, Farida Khanam and Mukhles shaheb sat in their garden, sipping tea and talking to each other. During this time, they were very happy. Except sometimes, Farida would wake up at midnight and sit by herself. That was all. Mukhles shaheb knew, but he never let on.

One day, Mukhles shaheb returned from work with a sort of cousin—the son of a neighbouring family in the village where he grew up. The man was at least five or six years older than him. His name was Abdul Bashir. Farida had barely met anyone from her husband's family since her wedding. She was quite surprised when her husband brought someone home with him.

'Farida, Bashir Bhai's family and mine used to live next door to each other. Bashir Bhai's mother was very fond of me. I can't begin to tell you all the treats that Chachi-Amma used to feed me.'

'Why don't you two sit in the garden? I'll bring out the tea.'

'Are there any green tomatoes left in the garden? Or have they all ripened?'

'There are a few.'

'I'll go and get some. I brought back some shrimp. Cook it with green tomatoes. I bought a chicken too. Cook it in a light sauce with new potatoes and green chillies.'

'I don't have enough onions to cook all that. There's just two left, and those are kind of dried up.'

'Okay, why don't you make the tea, and I'll run to the corner store to pick up some onions.' Mukhles shaheb hurried out of the house for the onions but came right back. 'Do we have any puffed rice in the house? You could serve it with the tea. Or should I get some of that as well?'

'There's no puffed rice, but there's some flattened rice. I'll fry that up. You go. Why are you so jittery?'

Mukhles shaheb wilted a little at Farida's question, as if she had caught him out. He mumbled something unintelligible and practically fled. 'No, I'm not jittery. It's just that they were very caring towards me when I was a child. I've eaten at their house ...'

Farida felt an intense tenderness for the man. The poor thing; he had no real family to speak of, and so because someone had shown him affection ages ago, he was still grateful about it.

She saw Abdul Bashir for the first time as she walked from the bedroom to the kitchen. A very average-looking man. His complexion was quite dark, but he was tall. Farida reflexively pulled the end of her sari over her head when she saw him.

'*Assalamalaikum.*'

'*Walaikum Assalam,* Bhabi shaheb. What a lovely home you have!'

'It's good of you to come, Bhai Jan. Why don't you sit in the garden? I'll bring the tea there.'

'Where did Mukhles go?'

'He went to the shop. He'll be back right away.'

Farida put the water to boil in the kitchen and thought, her husband had brought home a guest, she should be as hospitable as she could. She soaked two fistfuls of chickpeas to cook with meat spices; it was one of Mukhles shaheb's favourite dishes.

That night, after their guest had departed, Mukhles shaheb talked to Farida about how Abdul Bashir's family had taken in an orphan like him. It was with Abdul Bashir's mother that he had experienced small examples of what form a mother's love could take.

A week later, Mukhles shaheb returned home from work an hour earlier than usual. He had dinner and then, taking his time, he broached the subject with Farida.

'I met Bashir Bhai yesterday. He came to my office. He said that he could still taste your cooking on his tongue.'

'Really? You didn't tell me that!'

'I didn't, hmm? Bashir Bhai has a huge import-export business in Chittagong, you know. He's an engineer by training, but he runs a business. He wants to expand to Dhaka. That's why he's here. He's staying in a hotel for now. But how long can a person live in a hotel, right? So, I mean, I made him an offer. Let him stay here, in our spare room, for a few months. He won't have to worry about his meals, and it will mean a little extra income for us. What do you think?'

It seemed like a good idea to Farida. Especially the bit about a little extra income. She happily agreed. 'Yes, of course, he can stay in the spare room. That room gets a lot of air ... Did he say how much he'd pay?'

'No, but it won't be bad. He's very generous.'

Farida had witnessed his generosity herself. On the first visit, Abdul Bashir had tucked a large amount into her hand as a token gift for seeing the new bride's face for the first time. At first, Farida hadn't wanted to take it.

'Take it, Bhabi. Think of it as a gift from your *bhashoor*, your elder brother-in-law. It would be disrespectful of you to not accept it.'

'Oh, go ahead and take it. Of course, Bashir Bhai is your bhashoor!'

Farida had smiled shyly as she took the money. Later, when she counted it out by herself, her eyes had widened. A hundred takas! Did anyone just give away that kind of money?

Farida believed that he would pay them well. Not only did she not object to her husband's proposal, she agreed eagerly, with a smile on her face.

--

Abdul Bashir came to live at their house on Kobi Jashimuddin Road one Tuesday morning with a single small, black suitcase. From that moment, Farida's life changed enormously. Initially, it was all a kind of game. As if Farida was a twentieth century Draupadi, the only difference being that she had two husbands instead of five. One husband was as virtuous as Yudhishthira; the other was virile like Arjuna.

For the first time since their wedding, Mukhles shaheb felt undaunted and unburdened. He felt elated and unremorseful about having rid himself of an enormous weight. But Farida was bowed down by a gigantic burden—submerged to her neck in sin, and in order to hide it all, as inflexible as steel, as sharp as knives. And in her effort to keep holding her head high, higher than was necessary, her ribs curved like sickle moons.

From the outside, their household had no flaws. Farida's days were spent in managing her simple, conventional life to perfection. Making breakfast, taking her shower within fifteen minutes of Mukhles shaheb's and Abdul Bashir shaheb's leaving after breakfast, tidying the clothes discarded by the men, tidying the house, doing the laundry, prepping for meals, strolling in the garden after the cooking was done, fancying a cup of tea now and then, and waiting for the men to come home. When they returned: serving them food, tending to them while they ate, boiling the water for the afternoon tea, serving tea and snacks, sweeping the floors ... the duties of running a household. The evenings too passed in simple, conventional rhythms. Except on some nights, in the dark hours when owls hooted ceaselessly, and bats grew bloodthirsty, Farida, in a daze, descended from their bed, opened the bedroom door like a woman possessed, startled at every single creak of the door hinge, and walked resolutely to the room in the north side of the house. The door to the north-facing room always stood open.

As soon as Farida left their bed, Mukhles shaheb would jerk awake and sit straight and unmoving in bed. His breathing grew rapid. He sat there until Farida returned, his head bowed with deep suffering. Apart from the sharp sound of his labouring breath, which sounded like a horse's wheeze, he seemed dead. The sound of Farida's returning footsteps would revive his lifeless body and, like a good boy, he would curl up and fall into a deep sleep. There would be no way to tell that moments ago, he had been caught in some death grip.

But there was one thing Farida could say with her head held high. Whether day or night, during waking hours, neither Farida nor Abdul Bashir had even once been overly familiar with each other—not even in the absence of Mukhles shaheb. They were mindful of showing that respect to Mukhles shaheb, and Farida was rigid about abiding by that rule.

--

Farida couldn't tell how long she had been sitting on the floor. One hour? Two? She could check if she just raised her head, but she didn't feel like it. Memories were piled inside her like a tower of neatly folded laundry. If one memory unfolded itself, the old smells, aches and disgust thus unleashed would make her sick to her stomach. Farida was scared of memories; she didn't want to let them near her. Who knows what else she might remember—Farida wiped her tears. She had wept enough. This was not how life could move forward. She had to deal with the situation again and bring it under her control. If Bashir had told Lovely everything—fine. Let everything come out into the open. She would see if someone could just swoop in and destroy the family she had built so slowly but surely. And if he could, well then, this family deserved her contempt.

Despite these thoughts, she chanted '*Subhanallah, subhanallah*' without pause in her head, praising Allah's perfection. Farida was now hoping that Lovely would come home even later—so that she had enough time to regain composure. She couldn't afford to show any weakness. This world was the devil to those who were soft.

Beauty entered her room and stood in front of the mirror. She had discovered her first grey hair two days ago. An innocent white strand near her earlobe. It wasn't very long, but then Beauty didn't wear her hair long. She stared at the grey hair for a long time. So evening had almost arrived. For some strange reason, it didn't make her sad in the slightest. Rather it made her feel a relief of sorts. Pretty or ugly would make no difference anymore. That she spent more hours than a day contained on her beauty regimen was merely a way to pass the time, nothing more. Although time passed anyway. Listening to music, watching movies, flipping through magazines, beauty care and sleep. Sometimes it felt as if twenty-four hours were hardly enough.

Today the hours dragged—nothing made them move faster, nothing. She didn't feel like doing any of her usual things. If only she could see the outside world through this mirror—what was Apa doing, where was she, who was she with? Beauty couldn't begin to imagine what was taking her so long. As far as she knew, Apa didn't have anyone in the outside world to spend time with. Was that true though? Because about Lovely—nothing could be said with any certainty. At least not by Beauty. Because the handful of dangerous incidents that had taken place in their family had been perpetrated by the girl who was apparently artless and ingenuous. Lovely might very well have a toy boy in the outside world. Although Beauty's heart didn't seem to agree. What if Lovely had met with an accident? The thought occurred to her, but she didn't feel worried. Beauty was mostly stunned by Farida Khanam's reaction. There was no shouting, no cursing, no threats. There was something fishy there; there had to be something going on. Perhaps Amma herself had sent Apa somewhere, and so she already knew that Apa was going to be late coming back. But then why did Amma almost break down her door that morning, trying to get her to go as well? No, nothing was adding up. Her mind was tying itself in knots; she needed to clear her head. Now was the chance to go into the bathroom and smoke up the ganja. That would be good. She would smoke in there and whistle to herself—Beauty smiled.

She looked at herself in the mirror again. She still wasn't bad-looking. At least she looked way better than her sister. Even after all this time, Beauty couldn't fathom why Riaz went sniffing after Apa instead of her. *Uff*, the two of them had been mooning around each other, lovesick. Riaz used to bring study notes, and they often set themselves up at the desk in Beauty's room. The door stood wide open during those times. Amma could have walked in at any moment; she never bothered to knock or give them advance warning. All their loving took place under the table. The day Beauty first figured it out, she was so panicked she had trouble breathing. She remembered the moment clearly. It had been two thirty in the afternoon. They had just finished lunch. Lovely and Riaz showed up at her room with the study notes.

'Why my room? I'm going to take a nap now. Apa, go to your own room.'

'I won't be able to come for a couple of days, Beauty. I just wanted to explain the topic today. Also, I have to return these study notes to the person I borrowed them from.'

Beauty replied, 'So give them back today. We don't need any study notes.'

'I need them,' said Lovely. 'Honest, it won't take too long. I'll just learn everything from him now, and copy it later.'

'Why can't you do it in your room?'

'Where can we sit in my room? The desk is so small, and then there's only one chair.'

Beauty had felt aggravated by that disruption to her afternoon siesta. Grumbling, she went to the bathroom. As she was about to come out, who knew why, she cracked open the bathroom door as quietly as she could and watched them furtively. As soon as she understood what she was seeing, her limbs turned to ice. Apa was kneeling on the ground, a ballpoint pen in one hand. Within a split second, Riaz leaned over and kissed her full on the lips. Then, without making a sound, he got up from his chair, walked to the door, and looked around stealthily. When he returned to the desk, he kissed her again, this time hard. And what Beauty saw then still curdled her stomach when she remembered it. Disgusting!

She saw Riaz's hand slip easily inside Lovely's kameez, and that shameless girl still sat on her heels, like in the *namaaz* pose. Beauty couldn't watch anymore. She shut the door. She stood at the basin and, once, twice, thrice, she splashed the back of her neck and her face with cold water. She felt no pleasure inside, but a burning pain and hatred. She had almost vomited. She couldn't figure out how she would bear to look at them when she went out. She had sat in the bathroom for a very long time.

When she had finally emerged, her nose was decidedly wrinkled. As if she had spotted a dead rat, or as if someone had held up a decomposed rat to her nose. She exited the bathroom, and without glancing at them, left the room altogether. As she wondered what she could do, where she could go, she felt a stubborn anger grow within. *Arrey*, it's my room, so why am I the one who left? I can kick those two out if I want. There should be a limit to sleaziness— her thoughts sounded exactly like Farida Khanam. Beauty returned to her room with a triumphant air.

'Are you done with your notes?'

'Almost done.' Riaz gulped as he answered. Lovely's head was lowered; she was gazing unblinking at the notes.

'Beauty, will you get me a glass of water?' Riaz asked.

'No.'

'Okay, I'll get it myself.' Riaz went off to get the water. Beauty plopped herself down noisily on a chair. Three chairs were arranged on three sides of the square desk. One side of the desk was pushed against the wall. Riaz had the middle chair. Lovely was sitting to his left. Lovely and Beauty were facing each other. Beauty still clearly recalled her thoughts and feelings from that moment. All she had said as she ground her teeth had been, 'How dare they! How dare they!'

Lovely had heard nothing. Lovely was barely in this world. It was doubtful that she would be able to tell even if lightning had struck right between her eyes.

Riaz returned with a glass of water like a man possessed. He placed the glass gently in front of Lovely. Beauty no longer recalled if he had said anything or not. All she remembered was that as Lovely raised the glass with trembling hands, it slipped and fell, smashed into smithereens. The sound drew in Farida Khanam, who scolded them, and then, saying, okay, enough education for now, she got rid of Riaz.

From then on, their dangerous game continued under the desk. Kissing under the table, playing footsie, grabbing each other's hands—they left nothing undone. Beauty was unable to sleep a wink on the days these things happened. Her throat was dry like parched wood. No matter how much water she chugged, her thirst wouldn't be quenched. What astonished her the most now was that those two fools thought she didn't have a clue. Was she the wooden door or the table covered in floral-printed plastic—an object without sense, without intelligence? When she thought of this, it not only astonished her, she felt humiliated. Her body burned in mortification. If Lovely had just come to her and opened up about their relationship, perhaps it wouldn't have burned so unbearably. But Lovely kept up her pretense, and the under-the-desk drama continued.

One day, after their love-play was over and Riaz had left, Lovely handed her the pornographic booklets by Rashomoy Gupta disguised as study notes. That was the day she realised that her seemingly wet-behind-the-ears older sister was a hundred times more cunning than she could ever be. She could buy Beauty at one bazaar and sell her at four. She witnessed a fierce self-loathing and frustration within herself. On that day, in that moment, Beauty decided that she was going to tell Farida Khanam about Lovely and Riaz, and she felt no remorse. She even rehearsed just what to tell her mother. There was no need to go into an elaborate buildup; it should be short and sweet.

Farida Khanam had been sitting in the cane chair in the back veranda that evening, sipping her tea. Rabeya's Ma was by her feet, cracking her toes for her. Beauty went and checked that Lovely's door was shut. She opened it softly and saw Lovely reading. She didn't announce her presence and quietly closed the door again. Then she went straight to the back veranda.

'Amma, I want to talk to you about something. Bua, go and make me a cup of tea.'

Farida Khanam understood that Beauty was trying to get rid of the maidservant. She herself was very conscious about things like that. She always had an eye out to make sure that the private affairs of the household never reached the household help. She gestured at Rabeya's Ma with her eyes to leave. Rabeya's Ma left the veranda very unwillingly. Beauty checked to see whether she really had left or was lurking behind the door.

'What's all this drama? What do you want to tell me?'

Beauty deliberately took her time. As if it was hurting her to tell or she was still hesitant about whether she should tell. But that wasn't true at all. She was dying to tell.

'Why are you gasping like that? What's happened?'

'Amma, I saw Apa ...'

Farida Khanam had been sipping her tea in a relaxed manner, with her feet up on the table. She sat up straight when she saw Beauty's hesitation, and then became even more attentive when she realised it had to do with Lovely. Her ears pricked up like a hare's. 'You saw Apa what ...? What is it?' She almost hissed.

'Yesterday I saw Apa and Riaz Bhai holding hands.'

Beauty didn't linger near Farida Khanam for another moment. Even though she was dying to witness the transforming topography of her mother's face.

--

Beauty was still standing immobile in front of the mirror. So many things had just surfaced and disappeared in her mind. Sometimes Beauty thought that she could have chosen to not tell Farida Khanam. At least *she* shouldn't have been the person to tell. Given the desperate speed with which their love was proceeding, Farida Khanam herself would have figured it out soon enough. That would have been better. She wouldn't have to deal with this constant unease that stuck to her like fish smell stuck to the tongue.

She forced herself away from the mirror. The day felt awry—it had been off from morning onwards. There was no serenity. She pushed thoughts of Lovely out of her head before they had a chance to return. Let everyone go to hell, what did she care!

Slowly, Beauty walked towards the bathroom. Then a thought struck her, and she headed for the kitchen instead. Rabeya's Ma was sweeping the floor. The delicate aroma of hilsa fish was swirling in the air. The servants must have just finished eating.

'Where's that boy?'

'He's with your Abba. Giving the back of his neck a massage. I haven't been able to get him to do anything today.'

'Did Amma tell you to make the lentil paste?'

'No, she didn't.'

'It's finished. Make some more.'

'Okay.'

Beauty went back to her room and locked the door. She pulled out one of the marijuana sticks from behind her mirror, and went straight to the bathroom. She pulled out a matchbox from her bra and lit up, pulling on it deeply. Immediately, a tingling numbness spread throughout her body. Ah, bliss! She pulled down the lid and settled herself comfortably on the toilet. She alternated between short puffs and long drags, finishing half the stick pretty quickly. She saved the rest for later. That was some good stuff. She sat quietly on the toilet for a very long time.

She didn't know why she loathed Mukhles shaheb. But as far back as she could remember, she had always felt a distaste for him, even as a child. She didn't know where this distaste was born. With the kind of conciliatory life he led, as his child, it would have been normal for Beauty to feel tenderness towards him. The man had spent his entire life obeying his wife's every word. Obeying in blind faith, like diktats from God—without question, without complaint. Perhaps that was why she felt such hatred. Or perhaps there was some other reason, some reason that was beyond her understanding but within reach of her feelings. She faced this immense question as she sat on the toilet, and it felt good to reflect. She thought she could easily spend another hour just thinking through this question.

--

Farida was dozing off as she sat on the floor. She pulled herself together as concern about whether she had missed the time for the *Asr* prayers hit her. She pushed herself up. She even had a banal thought—she should drink some tea if she didn't want to get a headache. She performed her pre-prayer ablutions and then her prayers. On other days, whenever she stood at prayer, a thousand thoughts crowded her head—she hadn't doled out the laundry detergent to Rabeya's Ma; that boy hadn't returned the change after buying eggs, she needed to knock his teeth out of his head; she had noticed the light in Lovely's room burning until very late last night, she had to find out what was going on ... As soon as she settled herself on the prayer mat, all these jumbled thoughts emerged. Today she mustered all her concentration to perform her *namaaz*. But Farida felt unsettled even after she had prayed.

She left her room to ask for tea. Out of habit, she looked at the clock and then just stared. Twenty past five. This was a disaster!

'Rabeya's Ma, heat the water for tea.'

'Khalamma, I'm just telling you, that boy hasn't done a stroke of work. He's been with Khalu Jan the entire day.'

Farida paid no attention to Rabeya's Ma. As she stood at the kitchen door, she noticed that Beauty's door was shut.

'Have you served tea to Khalu Jan yet?'

'No, I haven't.'

'Don't, not without asking me. It's not good for him to have more than two cups a day.'

'Okay.'

'Okay, make tea for everyone now.' Farida opened the freezer and counted out exactly six homemade frozen shingaras. 'Fry up these shingaras to serve with the tea.'

'Okay.'

Farida stood in front of Beauty's door and thought of banging on it, but then moved away without making a sound. She wouldn't be able to keep her head if Beauty began a pointless argument with her. The best thing right now would be to not engage with anyone at all.

The servant boy hadn't even cleaned the window grilles today—she headed for the veranda. Mukhles shaheb was fast asleep, his head drooping. His chin was almost touching his chest. The boy was curled up at the other end of the veranda, also asleep. She was about to shout, but then she lowered her voice. 'Picchi! Picchi!'

Although she kept her voice low, the boy scrambled up. She didn't want to wake Mukhles shaheb. The farther he could be kept from everything, the better. She raised a finger to her lips, telling the boy to keep quiet. She gestured to him to come away from the veranda, and walked out. 'You have no work to do, right?'

'I was with Khalu Jan, Khalamma.'

'So because Khalu Jan is taking a nap, you can sleep as well? Who are you, a prince?'

'No, I wasn't sleeping.'

'Go and wipe down all the window grilles with soap and water. How many times do I have to tell you?'

The boy seemed relieved to be able to get away from her. Farida lost the thread of her thought again. She couldn't remember why she had come out of her room. Step by step, she went back to the veranda. Mukhles shaheb was still asleep. She felt very lonely as she stood on the threshold. A complication had reared its head in her life today, a major complication. Her elder daughter had gone out of the house by herself for the first time, and fallen prey to a man who could raze her family to dust with just a few words. Farida decided that she wouldn't say a single word or ask Lovely anything when she came back. Definitely not today. And, if Allah willed it, perhaps Lovely wouldn't ask her anything either.

She really had had no time to figure out what to say. She could just bald-faced deny everything, but that would probably just complicate things even more. A man wouldn't just randomly claim such things without any reason. She would have to concoct some believable mixture of truth and lies—but she had no idea what that could be. She would have to stand in the dock in front of her family, and she could expect not a smidgen of sympathy from any of them.

She became aware of a lump in her throat; she was finding it difficult to swallow. She tried to clear her throat, once, then twice. The second time, Mukhles shaheb opened his eyes at the noise. When he spotted her in the doorway, he tried to stand up, like a schoolboy attempting to stand at attention. As if a strict headmistress would punish him with a kneel-down if he didn't. But his body didn't grant him permission to stand up. He seemed flummoxed.

'Want some tea?'

He was still dazed by sleep. He rubbed his eyes and stared at her.

'Well? Do you want some tea?'

'Yes, I do. Is Lovely back?' It was probably waking up so suddenly that made him lose his judgement. Otherwise, he never knowingly said anything remotely provocative. Farida responded in an astoundingly calm manner. She felt very satisfied with the equanimity of her own voice.

'No, she's not. She'll be back when it's time.'

'Yes, yes, she'll be back. Let's have some tea. I feel a headache coming on.' He managed to evade the topic. He had been forced to spend almost the entire day in the veranda today. Sitting in the cane chair for so many hours had cut off circulation around his waist and torso. As he stood up from the chair, he lurched, a little off-balance.

'What's wrong? Are you feeling dizzy?'

'No, no, it's just that I've been sitting for so long ...'

Mukhles shaheb sidestepped her and left the veranda. She followed him. The tea had already been served on the dining table. Six thin threads of steam wisped upwards from the freshly fried shingaras. Farida pulled out a chair, which scraped against the cement floor, making an awful grating noise. She sat down. Mukhles shaheb was careful in pulling his chair out. The sight of the shingaras on the table cheered him up.

'You've been sleeping since early afternoon. Go, wash your hands and face and freshen up a little,' Farida told him.

Mukhles shaheb didn't argue. He pushed back the chair to its original position, and went to wash up.

'Khalamma, should I call Beauty Apa? The shingaras will go cold.'

Farida thought for a moment. She wouldn't be able to deal with any noise right now. If she said, 'Call her', Rabeya's Ma would probably bang on Beauty's door for all she was worth.

'Leave her be. She's probably napping. She'll come out on her own in a while.' She added, 'Make some lentil paste for her.'

'Yes, Apa told me already.'

Mukhles shaheb did his best to make no noise as he sat at the table. His face still looked damp. Farida had been waiting for him. They ate two shingaras each. Each drank a full glass of water. Then they had their tea in tiny sips.

Farida tried to make household-related small talk, like she did every day.

'Have you decided when you want to go to your village?'

'My older cousin told me to start from here after he calls me. They're going to arrange for a buyer first and then call.'

'A buyer for what?'

'My grandfather owned some good arable land on which rice grows.'

'Why sell it right now? Keep it—it might be useful in the future.'

'All this time, they didn't want to give me any share there at all. If I don't go now, it'll just slip through my fingers. I won't be gone for long, at most four or five days.'

'So then let's all of us go together.'

Mukhles shaheb was silenced at Farida's proposal. He forgot to swallow his mouthful of tea. The Farida he knew had been changing rapidly since morning. So rapidly, that he was finding it hard to keep up with her transformation. In the forty-two years of their marriage, he had never heard such a proposal. Naturally, he had no clue what his reaction should be. He managed to gulp down his tea and put on an air of being appreciative.

'Can we go? Is there a place for us to stay there?' she asked again.

'There must be. I'll ask my cousin when he calls me.'

'Yes, do that.'

If Farida could just disappear with her two girls, that's what she would do now. The thought of going away for a while to stay in the village suited her quite well.

--

November 16, 2007. The day contained all the elements of a winter's day as it moved swiftly towards November 17. Evening had descended on House No. 115/3, Monipuripara. The piercing wails of a baby from somewhere far away mingled with the pale light and shadow of the evening. Nothing was clear—neither the light, nor the dark, nor the crying. A muted, pressing unease flowed in Farida's veins. She had been waiting by the bedroom window for quite a while now. She thought about sitting down on the cane chair by the window now and then, but she didn't.

The window overlooked a large portion of their alleyway. She was staring out. Night was falling. It's the nature of the night to intensify everything at least threefold. Fevers spike at night, aches increase, fears escalate, love soars. The same thing was happening with her. She was curled up in fear. The uncertainty of whether or not her daughter would return was ripping her apart. She didn't even feel like praying. A kind of numbness had swallowed her. She felt nothing, but at the same time, she felt everything.

She pierced passersby in the alleyway with her gaze. A rickshaw went by. Her body grew taut. A CNG three-wheeler. She stopped breathing. Another rickshaw. She stood stock-still. A black cab. Her entire body pushed up on her toes.

She had no sense of how much time passed. A three-wheeler was proceeding along the alley. She gazed at it hopelessly. As it sped past their gate, she released the breath she had been holding in. It went a little farther before jerking to a stop. Farida pledged all her happiness in her prayer: 'Allah, let it be Lovely. I ask for nothing more in life.'

Nobody climbed out for an eternity. Then, after a while, she spotted her daughter's familiar, weary silhouette. She descended from the vehicle with her head bowed, walked slowly to the gate, opened the smaller gate, and entered the house. She covered her head with her shawl. Farida saw it clearly: Lovely paused with her head bowed. That was all she saw before she dropped into the chair. She needed time to regain hold of herself. The horse that was racing inside her heart needed to be reined in little by little. If she pulled the reins tight too fast, they might snap.

The bell was ringing. The boy ran to her door.

'Khalamma, Boro Khala is back.'

Farida was still in her chair. She was finding it hard to engage with the moment.

'Come in.'

It took some effort to raise her head. She untied the clutch of keys from her sari end. The boy left the room. Now? What was going to happen now?

—

The boy's teeth, bared in a grin, were visible at the top of the stairs. Lovely was waiting and waiting, biting down on her lip. The boy skipped down the remaining steps. He ran his mouth while unlocking the gate.

'Boro Khala, you're back. I was so scared!'

Lovely got stuck at the word 'I'. Did that mean that nobody else in the house was scared? Should she feel relieved? Although it wasn't a good idea to be relieved so quick.

'Where's Amma?'

'She's home.'

Lovely couldn't think of anything else to ask him. To be honest, she wasn't really feeling the slightest bit of curiosity about anything right now. She desperately needed to go to the bathroom. She didn't feel like facing anyone at home. As she climbed up the stairs past the boy, she decided that she would head for her room and go straight into the bathroom.

('An excellent idea, Apumoni!')

'Did anyone ask for your opinion?' she admonished the man inside her head.

When she reached the second floor, the main door stood wide open, but no lights were burning inside. The landing was almost dark, which suited Lovely fine. She entered the house without alerting anyone. She had to cross her mother's bedroom to reach her own; the light was on inside, but there wasn't a peep out of Farida Khanam. Amma *had* to know she was back—why had she holed up in her room? She should have jumped on Lovely by now. And where was everyone else? Abba, Beauty? The house felt cold and numb. Lovely didn't glance left or right. She kept praying '*ya nafsi, ya nafsi*' with her head bowed, and slipped into her room. She sat down heavily on her bed. As if someone had carried her inert body to the bed and dumped it there. She exhaled loudly, the noise spreading her existence throughout the room. She didn't turn on the light, didn't close the door, didn't go to the bathroom. She just sat on the bed, although a bathroom visit had become urgent. Finally, after a while, she got up and went into the bathroom.

She washed her face for a very long time, rubbing off all the dust and grime from the park. She pulled out the knife hidden in her shalwar and unsheathed it. What a beautiful knife! Going out by herself today had been a success. If Beauty saw this, she would sparkle with joy. If she liked it too much, she might even gift the knife to Beauty. It was fine whichever one of them had it.

Lovely began considering where she could hide the knife. Maybe under the mattress. But if Rabeya's Ma spotted it while making the bed, there would be an uproar. Of course, if she pushed it right to the middle,

Rabeya's Ma would never discover it. Lovely decided that was the way to go.

Finally, she finished her pre-prayer ablutions. Now she could spend a long time on the prayer mat. It would take her a long time; she had to perform all the prayers she had missed through the day. That was good though—she could at least hope that Farida Khanam wouldn't attack her while she was praying.

When Lovely emerged from the bathroom, she couldn't find her bearings in the dark. She could turn the light on, of course, but she didn't feel like it. Only Allah and Farida Khanam knew what terrible punishment awaited her. This veil of darkness seemed the best thing for now.

In the dark, she pulled open the top drawer of her dressing table, and hid the knife under the jumble of things for the moment. The safest thing to do right now was to stand in prayer. Somebody had told her once that it wasn't acceptable to perform your *namaaz* in the dark—who could it have been? It must have been Farida Khanam. The memory made Lovely hesitate. In the end, she turned on the light before standing on the prayer mat. What was the worst that could happen, after all—Amma couldn't kill her! Although it might have been better than this if she did kill her.

As she sat in prayer, Lovely wanted to surrender herself to Allah in the true sense of the word. As she prayed, she realised that Beauty had entered the room and was sitting on her bed. She still had many *rakats* of prayer left. But Beauty didn't lose her patience. When she turned her head to do the *salam*, she saw that Beauty was lost to the world, her head bowed. She didn't even notice Lovely watching her from the prayer mat.

After almost forty minutes, Lovely began her *monajat*. She raised her hands to Allah, but couldn't ask Him for anything. Suddenly she whispered, 'Allah, please let Amma like the red fabric.' After sitting for a minute with a mind devoid of thought, she finished her *monajat*. She turned her head while still on the prayer mat and looked at Beauty. She was still waiting there, in the same position.

'Where's Amma?' she asked.

There was no response. For the last few months, Beauty had seemed preoccupied like this quite often. Perhaps today she had been through a lot. Perhaps Farida Khanam had taken out all her rage on Beauty.

'Where's Amma?'

This time Beauty raised her head to look at her.

'Where have *you* been?'

'Ramna Park.'

'Are you kidding me?'

'Why would I do that? It's the truth.'

Beauty wanted to determine that it really was the truth just by looking at Lovely. She narrowed her eyes and stared at her sister.

'Do you even know where Ramna Park is? Do you know how to get there? You're just talking garbage.'

'Why would I need to know? I just asked the CNG driver to take me there.'

Lovely got up from her prayers and folded the prayer mat before hanging it on the clothing rack. Beauty remained seated on the bed, following her sister with her eyes. She was sensing a vital transformation in her sister. Could the outside air wreak such a change in just a few hours? A girl who was timid, who always seemed to be standing on shaky ground, was now looking her straight in the eye, claiming that she had gone to Ramna Park. Did she have any idea what would happen to her if Farida Khanam found out? The thoughts churned through Beauty's mind as she watched her sister. The more she thought about it, the more she wanted to die from shame and self-loathing. She was worse than Lovely—dumb, useless. Her eyes turned white. She wanted to rush over and rip Lovely's eyes and face to ribbons.

Lovely could tell that her sister was tracking her movements. It had been at least an hour and a half that she had been back—yet no sign of Farida Khanam so far. She was beyond astonished. She walked to her door in slow steps and peeked outside. The kitchen light was on, but there was nobody in the dining room, meaning there was nobody anywhere that Lovely could see. Perhaps, like in a horror movie, it would be the moment when she was most disarmed that someone would smash her head against the ground and hold her down. The surprising thing was that even though these thoughts trundled through her mind, she wasn't the least bit frightened. It was merely a feeling of loss that engulfed her.

Lovely moved away from the door. She stood in front of the dressing table mirror, taking her time undoing her braids.

'How did you dare pull off something like this?' They weren't words emerging from Beauty's mouth, but blades of flame. The flame almost licked Lovely—she felt the heat—but it couldn't burn her.

'Dare what?'

'Went out in the morning, came back in the evening.'

Lovely didn't have the slightest desire to talk to Beauty. She unwound her braids in slow motion; the entire house was reeling around her in slow motion. She was fast losing interest in finding out how everyone had fared through the day in her absence, why Farida Khanam still wasn't coming after her, when her imprisonment would begin, or whether some new punishment was being devised for today's infractions. However, she desperately wanted Beauty to leave her room.

'Beauty, I've got a headache coming on. Can you please go? I'm going to lie down with the lights turned out.'

'What?'

'I'm going to turn out the lights and go to bed.'

Beauty was stupefied at her audacity. First, this girl who had never stepped foot outside of the house by herself had gone out on her own; then, she had returned when she pleased, in the late evening; and now, she was behaving as if she didn't give a shit about anybody. Suddenly, her fury made her lose all control. She jumped off the bed, stamping her foot like a horse, and began to scream. 'You *will* tell me where you've been right now. Right now! I've never gone anywhere, and you'll just roam around the city as you please! What is this, a free for all? Amma hasn't said a word to you yet, why? Was it Amma who sent you somewhere? Where? Where did she send you?'

Lovely brushed her hair indifferently. She watched her sister's frenetic rage with disinterest. She even yawned. It was the yawn that did it. Beauty's frenzied outburst grew uncontrollable. She went berserk. She rampaged across the room, stopped, screamed something, snarled, then screamed some more.

'As if you've just saved the world by going out. Do I make you yawn? You're so stuck up, you'll learn your lesson now! I'll take you down a notch! Everyone thinks they can get away with anything! I'll show you. Oh, I'll show you!'

Beauty stopped storming around the room, then. Lovely was still in front of the dressing table. She turned around when she saw Beauty rushing at her like a hunted tiger. In the mirror, her freshly brushed hair spread like a wave over her back, in contrast with the stark white of Beauty's fierce eyes, her hair bushy like a lion's mane and her arms raised in a violent zeal. Beauty stopped dead when she saw herself in the mirror. Then, without another word, she turned around and ran from the room.

Beauty's screaming had brought Rabeya's Ma to the kitchen door. She held a rolling pin in her hand. The boy ran in from the veranda to witness the fun. But neither Farida Khanam nor Mukhles shaheb came out.

Although Farida heard every single word of Beauty's outburst from her room, she didn't budge an inch. She remained sitting in the same chair. She didn't have the strength to face either of her daughters. She could tell that Beauty was about to direct her wrath at her. She could get up and shut her door if she wanted—but she didn't feel like it.

'Amma, I want to know what's happening in this house. Apa has been back for over an hour, and she's sitting in her room comfortably, brushing her hair, rubbing cream on her face—and you're hiding in your room! Why? Aren't you going to ask her where she was all this time, what she's been up to? Or did *you* send her somewhere? Where did you send her?'

'Get out of this room. Right now!'

'No, I won't. What are you going to do? As if I'm the one at fault for asking some fair questions. You won't say a word to your other daughter who's come home after doing who knows what—you're just going to shout at me. I want to know why you won't say anything to her.'

'Because I don't want to. Do I have to answer to you? I've done what I've done. I don't even have to answer to

Allah. I am the one to whom everyone else will answer. You little bitch, how dare you question me! Look at you. You devil! Creating all this drama in the house. Why don't you just die? Get out of my room, get out ...'

That wash of words churned out of the deepest core of Farida's soul like a river bursting its banks. Her volume barely reflected her rage and resentment. At that moment, it was as if the entire house froze and died. Beauty had been ready to counterattack, but after a glimpse of Farida's face, she turned tail and left the room quietly. Farida shut the door.

As she stood in the dining room outside her mother's door, Beauty felt as if she was alone, friendless, in the middle of a vast plain. The plain was closing in on her slowly, but fast enough so that she could tell what was happening. Soon she would disappear in the field, in the grass, in the air. Desperately, she looked this way and that, and noticed Mukhles shaheb standing behind the veranda door, watching her. And she was pretty sure that the boy was standing right beside him. She realised that everyone was watching her from different rooms. Lovely's door was nearly shut, but she could swear Lovely's entire attention was now focused on her. Beauty's fury flew towards Mukhles shaheb. Was this mealy-mouthed man really her father? This slimy, slithery man—Beauty felt nauseated.

'What are you doing behind that door? You're useless, but you have to shove your nose into everything. You're just a ...'

'Beauty, I'll smash your face in. Is that how you speak to your Abba? You animal!' Farida Khanam roared at her from inside her room.

Beauty immediately shut up. She glared at Mukhles shaheb, who still stood behind the veranda door, her eyes burning. She couldn't see his face; she could only see his swaying shawl. Finally, he shifted, disappearing along with his shawl. Beauty went back to her room and locked the door. But she wasn't noisy this time like she usually was—she didn't slam the door shut or rattle the bolt. She tiptoed all the way, and was careful enough to be quiet when she slid the bolt. As if a terminal patient was asleep in the household—sleeping a sleep that could be broken at the slightest noise, and sleep that was imperative for their survival.

Rabeya's Ma was terrified. She had rolled out four or five whole-wheat rutis for the master; to be made fresh when they sat down to eat so they were piping hot. Right now, she had nothing else to do. The whole house was as cold as the grave. So quiet that from the kitchen she could hear the constant chirping of crickets in the veranda. They stopped momentarily before starting up again.

She thought of going and shutting the veranda door. Mukhles shaheb had settled himself in the living room a little while ago. He had probably been feeling cold in the veranda. He had his warm shawl wrapped tightly around his head and torso. Farida Khanam would definitely have a fit if she spotted the veranda door standing open. But for the life of her, Rabeya's Ma couldn't make herself go there. Something was going on today—there were bad smells everywhere, and every so often she got the chills. The boy was sitting quietly beside her. He was cold too; his limbs were freezing, and he kept worrying that someone would show up to give him a good thumping.

Rabeya's Ma couldn't figure out whether to serve dinner or not. It would take a little time to warm everything up. She needed to cook the rutis. She was distraught and bewildered.

'Hey, boy, get up. Go and set the table.'

'Nobody's going to eat tonight.'

'They won't?'

'They won't.'

'What are we supposed to do? I'm hungry.'

'So am I.'

The two of them waited in the kitchen with hunger in their bellies. After a while, they dozed. Neither knew how much time had passed. But they could tell that the night was deepening. It was a winter's night; it shrouded itself in fog.

Farida's door was swung wide open. She pushed herself to behave normally, like any other day. She found Rabeya's Ma and the boy snoozing on entering the kitchen. Rabeya's Ma's head was resting against the wall. The boy had propped his arms on his knees with his head hung between them. Farida stared at them for a moment before calling them awake.

'Rabeya's Ma, serve dinner.'

Rabeya's Ma's head jerked up, and she scrambled herself to a sitting position. The boy stood up.

'Set the table, bring water for everyone. Be quick, it's very late.'

The boy seemed in no hurry. But Rabeya's Ma bustled around. With sleepy eyes, she turned the stove on and placed the flat skillet on it to cook the rutis. She was suddenly freezing. She wrapped her shawl tightly around herself. The cold was making her hunch her shoulders. Periodically she held her palms over the hot pan, rubbing them against each other. Farida worked alongside Rabeya's Ma. She turned on two more burners and began warming up the other dishes. She didn't just issue orders and leave the kitchen; she stood there and supervised.

'Rabeya's Ma, slice up a lemon. Hey, you, boy—'

'Yes?'

'Set a plate for the bones. I have to remind you every God-given day.'

The boy nodded and returned to the dining room. Farida stayed in the kitchen and shouted to the boy to call Mukhles shaheb to dinner. She warmed the duck curry and the red rice herself, and served it in the dishes. Rabeya's Ma delivered them to the table. Farida whipped up a quick raita, mixing finely diced cucumber with tart yogurt.

When she was done, she went to the dining room to find Mukhles shaheb waiting quietly in his chair. Their eyes met, but neither spoke. Farida knocked lightly on Lovely's door first, then on Beauty's.

'Lovely, come out to eat. Beauty, aren't you going to have dinner? Come on.'

As soon as Farida moved away from the doors, the girls came out. As if they had been waiting all this time with their backs against their doors, emerging as soon as they were called. Their faces gave away nothing of what was going on inside either of them. They sat in their usual seats like any other day. Lovely was face to face with Farida for the first time since she had returned. But neither Farida nor Lovely uttered a single word on the subject. Everyone behaved as usual.

Lovely's head wasn't working properly. Normally, by now her limbs should have curled up and retracted into her belly out of sheer terror. She had completely forgotten that she should keep up a guilty demeanour. Hunger and thirst had left her desperate. As soon as they began to eat, she nearly pounced on the food. There was no chitchat while they ate. Farida Khanam didn't even try to make her usual mealtime household-related small talk. Four tired people sat on four chairs, with their heads bowed, wolfing everything down.

Mukhles shaheb could only think of food and stretching himself out on his bed. He had been in a precarious mental state all day; he felt like he was a worm, or something close to it.

Beauty was concentrating on chewing duck bones. She couldn't care less even if the world came to an end right this second.

Farida was eating, but she couldn't taste anything. She had made a decision after Lovely's return, so she was feeling somewhat lighter now. She had decided to tell her daughters about Abdul Bashir. Lovely already knew the story; nevertheless, she would sit both of them down and tell them. She would give them strict instructions beforehand that neither of them was to interrupt with needless questions or talk over her while she was speaking. If they had anything to say, she would listen to them after she was done. But not tonight—they all needed this night to recover themselves.

Lovely was eating, but everything happening around her seemed a blur. As if she was sitting by an open window inside a train rushing at an incredible speed, and the scenery outside was constantly moving farther and farther away, leaving her behind. She could feel the outside world, but she couldn't comprehend it.

Dinner over, one by one, they retired to their bedrooms and locked their doors. Each of them hunched a little lower as they stood up from their chairs. An unbearable pressure on their shoulders did its best to push them to the ground. Their mental state oozed itself into the very house.

—

It was almost a quarter past midnight. The fog that was slathered across the alleys gradually grew thicker. It grew so dense that finally it surrounded the house completely, making it vanish. Even the intense searchlight of the winter's moon failed to uncover the house. Lovely pulled out the knife from her drawer. She had to place it under her mattress. But she wanted to sharpen it before she hid it again. Enchanted, she tested the knife's sharpness. She gently stroked the stainless-steel blade with her right index. The icy feel of the blade in her hand made her tremble to her core.

('Apumoni, what are you up to?')

'Where were you all this time?'

('I was asleep. Who are you waiting for?')

'For Beauty.'

('She's not coming. She's fallen asleep.')

'She will.'

('What will you do if she comes?')

'Play.'

('Just forget about this game business tonight. Get some rest. You've had quite a day.')

Lovely was amused. The man inside her head was scared of her. This was a first for her, where the strings were in her hands; she would pull and they would dance.

Lines from a song suddenly grew in her head like a vine: *Amar mone ki anondo, amar mone ki anondo, tumi khawailey ami khai, Allah, tumi khawailey* ... What joy in my heart, what joy in my heart, I only eat, Allah, if you feed me ... And she began laughing so hard that she nearly choked. The man inside her head laughed raucously with her, as if they were competing. She swallowed the laughter just as suddenly.

('Apumoni, someone's listening by the door.')

'I know. It's Beauty.'

('Aren't you going to open up? Of course, you don't have to. She'll just wait awhile and go away.')

There was a knock on the door. So soft, that it would be hard to hear unless someone was listening for it. Lovely heard it the first time. She got up. She put the knife down on the table, but picked it up again, slipping it under her pillow before going to the door.

('Apumoni, don't open the door. Let's just get into bed tonight and have fun. Whoever's waiting will wait and then leave.')

Lovely walked implacably to the door and opened it. Beauty stood there. The light from the room slid over Lovely's right shoulder and illuminated half of Beauty's face; the other half remained in darkness. The two of them stood facing each other. Neither shifted a hair's breadth for the other.

'Move, Apa, let me in.'

'Why?'

('You're right. What does she want in this room so late at night?')

'I will not quarrel with you, I swear.' Beauty recited the words just as she used to when they were children.

Lovely didn't budge. Beauty shifted a little and entered the room, brushing against her. Lovely didn't close the door; she went and sat on her bed. Then she placed a hand lightly on her pillow. She couldn't decide whether to show Beauty the knife or not.

'Aren't you going to go to sleep?'

'I'm not sleepy. Apa, do you want to play?'

'No.'

Beauty blazed at the rejection. 'Why won't you play?'

'I've been walking around all day. I'm sleepy.'

Beauty glared at her. Lovely drew back further. She shifted a little closer to her pillow.

'You're not sleepy.'

She trembled at Beauty's words. The fingers of her right hand became restive on the pillow.

'What's under the pillow?'

('Damn!')

'What's under the pillow, Apa?'

When she tried to answer, Lovely realised that her throat was parched. She cleared it noisily. 'Nothing much; a knife. I bought it from New Market today.'

Lovely left her bed and went to the dining room. She poured some water from the jug on the dining table and drank a full glass of water.

('Apumoni, have another glass for me. Let's cool down.')

'Why aren't you asleep?'

('How can I sleep if you don't go to sleep?')

'If you're not going to sleep, then be quiet.'

Lovely poured out another glass of water and carried it back to her room. Beauty was waiting with the knife in hand. When she saw Lovely enter, the lip she had bitten down on stretched into a smile. Lovely shut the door with one hand and slid the bolt. She placed the glass of water exactly in the middle of the small table in the middle of the room. She didn't look in any other direction. She tried her best to pull out a chair and sit down without making any noise; she gestured at Beauty to sit down as well in the chair across from her.

'Tonight, we'll play with a real knife, right, Apa?' Beauty spoke in a young-girl voice. Suddenly she was feeling happy for no reason. She was even feeling fond of her sister. She dropped into the chair across from Lovely. She balanced the knife on the rim of the water glass.

'Hmm.'

('Apumoni, you're completely out of it tonight. You're going to take a licking if you play.')

'Where did Amma send you? You *have* to tell me.' Beauty's eyes did not leave the knife. She stared at it, enamoured.

'Nobody sent me anywhere, I told you. I went from Gausia Market to Ramna Park.'

'The person who's never been out by herself, just went off to visit Ramna Park? You just tell me whatever, and I'm supposed to believe it?'

'If you don't, you don't. I'm just telling you what happened. I met a guy there. He brought me back home.'

Beauty seesawed between belief and disbelief. Perhaps Lovely really had gone to Ramna Park. But that last bit was just made up.

'If Amma didn't send you ... but then you came home so late. Amma should have eaten you up alive but ... just tell me the truth, Apa. I promise I won't tell anyone.' Beauty had barely finished her words before she began chuckling.

Lovely looked at her, startled, but didn't say anything.

'Our brains are addled,' continued Beauty. '*Arrey*, who am I going to tell? Do I have anyone to tell? Who did you meet? Some guy? And he brought you home? Hah!' The scorn in her voice twisted her neck. Her manic sniggering returned, like a bout of coughing.

Lovely stared at Beauty for a very long time. Why, couldn't she meet or be friendly with someone? Had Beauty forgotten that it was her Riaz had liked, *her*.

('Apumoni, forget this old saga. She's said one thing that's right on the money though—we came home in the evening, and we're still alive and healthy. What's the deal here?')

This was a mystery that Lovely had been trying to solve since she had returned. Not only had Farida Khanam avoided asking her where she had been, it almost felt like she was steering clear of her. She hadn't even looked her directly in the eye. Did this mean that from now on she could come and go as she pleased? That she didn't have to be mindful of anyone? It was all just castles in the air, but still Lovely felt a remarkable strength within herself. She looked at Beauty and saw that her neck was still twisted, and that ugly smirk still clung to her lips like a smear of spit. Beauty was due for a hard lesson.

('You're back to thinking about Beauty again. Think about why your mother isn't coming after you. There's something fishy there.')

'I don't care two cents about that,' Lovely responded to the man inside her head, and picked up the knife. The feel of the cold steel in her fist made her shiver. She tried to loosen her grip, but instead clasped it tighter.

'Apa, want to play?'

'No.'

'I don't want to play either.'

'Tonight, I'm going to be Amma, and you're going to be me,' Lovely said.

'I told you, I don't want to play.'

'I'm late coming home, so Amma is going to get the whole story out of me, and then lock me up ... No, she's not going to lock me up—she's going to kill me.'

'No, I'm going to be Amma, and you're just going to stay you. Let me ...'

Beauty tried to snatch the knife, but Lovely held it in a strong grip.

'No, I'm Amma. Where were you all this time?' Lovely mimicked Farida Khanam exactly.

Beauty recoiled at the fierce scolding, but she didn't lose the thread of the game. She regained control of herself almost immediately and responded in a gentle voice, just like Lovely: 'I went to Gausia.'

'I told you, I didn't go to Gausia, I went to Ramna Park. If you're going to play, then play properly, otherwise don't bother.'

'Why did you go to Ramna Park?'

'Why are you asking that? I'm supposed to ask you that.' Lovely was a different person today. Today was the day for everyone to be what they weren't, or perhaps to be what they were.

'Why did you go to Ramna Park?'

'I don't know. To just hang out.' Beauty began to focus on the game. She was forgetting all the rules; she couldn't make any more mistakes.

'To hang out? Who did you go there with? I'm going to kill you today. I'm going to take care of your whoring once and for all.' Lovely furrowed her brows. Each word was forced through clenched teeth.

'I didn't go with anyone. Who am I supposed to go with?'

'You slut, I'm going to punish the two of you so that you're stuck indoors, crippled, for the rest of your lives!'

'We're already crippled.' As soon as Beauty had uttered those words, she grabbed the knife from Lovely and stood up. She did it so fast that Lovely was completely caught unawares. Beauty waved the knife dangerously close to

Lovely's eyes. 'Who's going to punish who now? Cripple us! In your dreams!'

Lovely swivelled her neck to get away from the knife and, at the same time, she tried to shove her chair backwards with her feet.

'Remember, I know everything. I know everything about everyone. I'll show you! Kissing and making out right under my nose. That bastard, giving me the brush-off, rejecting my kisses. Why, was my tongue covered in poison-spit and yours was all honey, honey, honey?'

Lovely leapt up from her chair. Beauty had been crouching over Lovely with the knife, her body curved like the sickle moon. When Lovely jumped up so suddenly, Beauty lost her balance and leaned onto the empty chair, the knife sliding out of her hand and falling to the floor. The steel rang against the cement. Beauty grabbed hold of the chair back, steadying herself; then she picked up the knife and put it on the table.

Both sisters were panting with their mouths open. Both felt deprived of air. Beauty sat down on the chair; she had lost control of her limbs. She spilled water as she tried to raise the glass to her lips.

'Go get your own water, Beauty. I brought this glass for myself.'

Beauty paid no attention and drank it all up. Sated, she looked at her sister and smiled. An easy, familiar smile. She held out the glass with the last of the water towards Lovely. Lovely ignored the outstretched hand. She pulled the other chair very close to Beauty and sat down quietly. Beauty put the glass down beside the knife indifferently.

'So you're the one who told Amma about Riaz. I'd thought it was that boy.'

Beauty grinned. Lovely didn't look at her even once. Lazily, she looked at the glass and the few sips resting at the bottom with her head lowered.

—

We don't know exactly how long Lovely stared at the glass. All we know is that like a fish striking suddenly and disturbing the calm surface of a pond, something unfamiliar struck Lovely's inner heart.

We see Lovely picking up the knife from the table in a motion slower than time. When she picks it up, she also grabs a part of the rucked-up plastic tablecloth. But then she stops and releases it awkwardly, and in her clasp, the knife trembles in hesitation. For a fraction of a moment, the knife leaves the custody of her fingers, but is immediately imprisoned in her hard grip. The movement topples the glass. Drops of water roll across the plastic tablecloth like glass marbles, then reach the edge of the table, and begin to drip onto the floor. Beauty's nearly shut eyes startle; at first her eyes close, but then they widen. Her gaze is as unshifting as the white of a riverine island, as the light of a half moon, as the headlights of a night train stalled for eternity.

The numb silence of the winter's night closed in on them. Beauty's one arm swayed in the air; the other arm lay on the table. Then her head rested carelessly on that arm. Her black hair, tended with such care, spread like a wave across her back. The hint of a smile was barely visible at the corner of her mouth. She looked a little embarrassed at having screamed so loud. It was unclear whether her eyes reflected surprise or admiration at her sister's accomplishment.

Someone was banging hard on the closed door. The sound pierced Lovely's ears, her brain, her heart, but still didn't reach inside her.

The banging was so loud, it was as if they wanted to pulverise the door, blow it away. Then, at some point, the storm died down. Peace. Lovely shoved the chair back. It didn't work; the chair slid a hair's breadth to the side, and Beauty's hair touched her elbow. Soft and smooth. This could be a great advertisement for Sunsilk shampoo, thought Lovely. Not once did she look squarely at Beauty. The yellow glow from the tube-light behind Beauty's head was dissolving. Unbearably intense, the sticky, molten light oozed down the walls towards her along with the odour of scorched hair.

For the longest time, Lovely couldn't tell what felt so sticky under her feet. The moment her left big toe touched the cold, metallic liquid, her stomach turned. The fluid clung to the soles of her feet with a fierce loyalty.

Her body repulsed, her nose wrinkled; she felt helpless in some way. She really needed a drink of water right now.

She stared at Beauty for a little while. Or perhaps for a long time. She picked up the arm hanging in midair, and placed it on the table. Beauty lay with her head on the table in such a peaceful manner—Lovely felt great tenderness for her.

She stood up from the chair quite capably. Her head didn't feel dizzy; however, she had a bit of a moment with her arms. At first, they hung by her sides. But soon her right hand rose to her chest. The left hand tried to follow the right and got into trouble. The thumping of her heart had grown so laughably urgent that her poor hands didn't feel very comfortable on her chest. Lovely thought of resting them on her waist. That would give her a fairly straight-backed appearance; at this moment, appearance was of paramount importance. But it didn't work—every time she placed her hands on her waist, they slid off. After four tries, she gave up. Finally, she placed them behind her back and held the index and middle finger of her left hand tightly with her right.

Lovely stood unmoving for the next fifty-four minutes; and in those fifty-four minutes, her entire existence swirled around her. The swirling began at the soles of her feet and moved towards her head, but it never reached there—it grabbed her by the throat. When she was almost strangled, it let her go and began spiralling its way downwards again. Then it made its way up again, down again, up, down, up ...

In those fifty-four minutes, Lovely was born; when she was three years old, Beauty was born, with a full head of hair. How fair she was! As disconcerting as the unexpected first light of dawn in a room where the curtains have been drawn. Outside, the sound of Farida Khanam turning the key, the smell of egg in Beauty's hair, opening the door and rushing out to the rooftop, Mukhles shaheb gently swaying to the beat of the song, *Kabhi kabhi mere dil mein khayal aata hai/ke jaise ... Sometimes the thought occurs in my heart /I wonder ...* And Riaz and Red-muffler guy and the man inside her head.

Lovely searched every nook and cranny inside herself for the man inside her head. She even whispered to him once: 'Are you there? Can you hear me?' But the man was nowhere to be found. He had disappeared of his own free will, just as he had once appeared of his own free will. At first, she felt sad, but then she was a little annoyed. Of all the times to leave!

Lovely stood still no longer; she opened the door and stepped out. Only a thin shaft of light fell into the dining room; otherwise the place was quite dark save for the zero-watt lightbulb. She stood in the doorway and looked in both directions. She liked listening to the sound of her own heavy breathing. It gave her a different sort of confidence: no, there was nothing to fear.

Lovely shut her bedroom door with the greatest care before turning towards Farida Khanam's room. She took one or even two steps that way, but then came back. She stood by the kitchen door with her ears pricked. Then she locked it from the outside, and walked towards Farida Khanam's room.

Now Lovely was standing at Farida Khanam's door, knocking very gently. She was following a certain rhythm: knock-knock, knock-knock, knock-knock.

The door opened. There was a zero-watt lightbulb burning in Farida's room too. Her face was a blur. At first, Farida couldn't tell who it was. When she tried to speak, she realised that her voice wasn't loud enough.

'Who is it? What? What do you want so late, Lovely? Go to sleep.'

'I won't be able to sleep tonight, Amma.'

'That's fine, just go and lie down. Go.'

'Is the shovel from the garden in the upstairs landing? Give me the keys.'

'What?'

'I killed Beauty, Amma. You don't have to come. I can take care of everything myself.'